INSIDE
THE GOLD-PLATED
PISTOL

by
Cynthia Bruchman

Published 2019

Printed in the United States of America
Print ISBN: 978-1-951490-16-4

Publisher Information:
DartFrog Books
4697 Main Street
Manchester Center, VT 05255

www.DartFrogBooks.com

CHAPTER ONE

SALLY

1928

A t the Liberty Theatre in Jerome, Arizona, Sally counted twenty-five faceless heads in the dimmed house. The seats rose steeply. Each row held a dozen, and the house held a hundred comfortably. Upstage, two Kliegl lamps lit the back screen blue. In the wing, she locked arms with her dance troupe, the Copper Cuties, while Leo tapped the piano keys to the song "Ain't She Sweet." His long thighs bounced along with the introduction. On the third beat of the reprise, Sally nudged her four dance partners onto the stage. The yellow tutus rustled, and their black-hosed legs crossed and kicked. This was the first performance of the new routine she had choreographed, inspired from a recent article in *McCall's* magazine. She had read the article seven times, staring at the pictures of the kicking squad of precision dancers, a line of long-legged symmetry, chins up, poised. They were called the Rockettes and were growing so popular, the article claimed, they were taking their show to New York City.

The ache to be in the front row, to see them kick, to hear their tap shoes click-clack on the stage, to listen to the orchestra play—*Oh!* her heart ached. She thought she might break down and ask her mother to pay for a ticket to see them. She refrained. Her mother would interpret the request as a sign of reconciliation and would want to travel with her. The two-hour show would be heaven, but not worth journeying across the country in a train with her mother. She'd be trapped and forced to endure the kaleidoscope expressions of Connie Vandenberg's face. First would come the tears, then the tantrum, followed by threats, and finally, the sullen dismissal telling Sally to "Go to hell." *Yes,* Sally decided, *better to imagine the show.*

Sally listened to the taps of shoes in sync to the melody of "Ain't She Sweet." She had squealed anytime she'd heard it on the radio and given Leo the money to obtain the sheet music to Ben Bernie's new song. She'd then forced Leo to play it repeatedly until she'd memorized the lyrics. The ensemble from Jerome agreed to her idea to imitate the Rockettes. Sally bartered yellow netting and cheap silk fabric from Mr. Sang in exchange for a pair of opal earrings, an apology gift from her mother two years ago. Opals! What did she care about opals? She wanted Connie Vandenberg's emerald and diamond collection. How many years would she have to wait before she inherited her mother's stash of jewels? Sally's tap shoes smacked the wooden floorboards harder and looked again at their matching costumes. The Chinese tailor and his son turned the material into five outfits. When the Copper Cuties put them on, Sally realized they looked like bumblebees. *Shit.*

All of these thoughts spun in her mind in rapid succession during the first turn on stage.

She imagined the Rockettes. Her smile grew wider. The house was dark, and the fog of cigarette smoke reflected two spotlights aimed at them. One of her dancers was short and waddled. A couple of the girls were mediocre, and Sally was disappointed they couldn't kick high with their toes out in front of their chins. She looked to her left, and, with the footlights hot at her feet, she looked to her right. The song ended and some of the men clapped. One stood up and whistled.

"Let's see ya shimmy!"

Sally recognized Luke Foster. He came every Wednesday to see them dance, zozzled after drinking for hours beforehand.

Leo began a long introduction meant to showcase their tap-dancing ability. Sally was the only one who had formal training: five years of dance classes paid for by her mother in Chicago. The four dancers circled Sally, hiding her behind their tutus while she unfastened her own to reveal a black corset and black silk short-shorts. She pulled out Indian feathers of various colors attached to a headband from the waistband of her shorts and hurriedly slipped it on. The Copper Cuties opened the circle and passed Sally's tutu behind their backs to the wing while Sally click-clacked forward. Downstage center, she posed with arms open and with one leg bent at the knee; she grinned with enthusiasm. She was particularly proud of this onstage dress change. She had seen it in New York when Connie took her to see the Ziegfeld Follies. That's when her mother gave Sally the opal set as an apology gift. How ridiculous to think sending her father away most of her life was acceptable and that two black opals from Australia would make up for lost time? She wanted to spit at Connie Vandenberg. Watching the Ziegfeld Follies had been tainted, which was just one more justification for Sally to run away to her Aunt's boarding house and speakeasy in Jerome, Arizona.

"Come on, Dotty," Sally whispered to the lumpy last-minute acquisition after one of the original Copper Cuties disappeared last week. "Our tips depend on your wiggle."

They posed and jiggled their hips in tune to Leo's piano playing, setting themselves for the transition to Jack Smith's "Me and My Shadow."

Their tap shoes echoed up the theater. *Stomp, step, step, kick, stomp. Side step, side step, turn, bend, and wiggle.* The men clapped and hooted.

Next, Sally performed a solo rendition of "Dance, dance, dance." Leo played a modified version, and Sally twirled and shuffled while the Copper Cuties provided a backdrop. Hands connected behind their backs, the troupe took two steps to the left then two to the right. They rocked until the end of the number. After the show, the five bumblebees walked up the backstairs to the dressing room. They took off their make-up, passed around cigarettes, and propped up their legs on the makeup table. Dotty rubbed her toes and thick ankles. Soon, she was ready to leave and waved good-bye. Dotty attempted to open the door, but Luke Foster leaned on the door frame, his eyes half-closed and hiccupped.

"Hey, hey, what's the hurry? You're Dot, right? Butt me, and let's go outside."

Dotty snorted. "Hit the road. I ain't interested."

Luke's upper lip curled. He pinched Dotty's cheeks. "What you so uppity for? You're just a hoofer."

Sally rose from her chair and crossed the room. Her cotton shift exposed her arms, and the hallway breeze made the hair on her forearms tingle. She did a two-step and put her arm through Luke Foster's elbow and spun him away from the dressing room.

She said, "Luke, I got a cigarette. Let's go smoke it." Luke tried to focus on Sally, then frowned at Dotty, and dismissed her with the flip of his middle finger.

Sally gave a warning look to Dotty to let it go. Dotty snorted and readjusted the strap on her shoulder. With the back of her hand, she wiped off the scent of him from her cheeks. Sally led Luke around the corner of the Liberty Theater to her aunt's hooch, called Bernie's. To window shoppers, it was a soda fountain and confectionery shop where chocolate egg creams, hard candy, and cigars were sold. That was the Prohibition cover up. Most of her customers preferred to visit the basement for bathtub gin drinks like the "Bee's Knees." When her aunt received a bootleg shipment of rum, she'd make a batch of Sally's favorite, the "Mary Pickford." Inside a coat closet and behind a camouflaged door, Sally led Luke to a side parlor with a small bar. She bought him a bourbon and told him she'd be back later. He looked at her confused but happy. He stared at the brown liquid in the glass. Sally stepped outside through an escape door to the side street. All was quiet.

The glowing moon lit up the alley well enough. She lit a cigarette and stared at it. Bushes rustled and someone stepped into view. Sally groaned and hoped it wasn't a soused miner. From the shadows, a tall figure approached. Sally wasn't sure if it was a female or male with long hair but guessed the beanpole was female. Sally watched her wipe her eyes with her wrist. The figure pulled back her hair and walked over to Sally and stood in the beam of the moonlight.

"They told me to look back here."

Sally said nothing.

"I watched your show. Are you Sally Vandenberg?"

"Who wants to know?"

"Her father. Jonathan Vandenberg sent me."

Sally lifted her eyes and sniffed, took a drag from her cigarette, and tossed it. "That's the funniest thing I've heard all week. What's an Indian like you know about Jonathan Vandenberg?"

Awkward and silent, the woman set her jaw and stood there.

Sally rolled her eyes at her expression and said, "Okay, okay. I'm Sally. Come on, follow me. I gotta turn in my money to my aunt, and then we'll have a chat."

They returned to Bernie's and walked past the soda jerk, Carl, who chewed a stogie and wiped the counter. At the end of the building, Sally lifted a trap door on the floor. Down the stairs into shadows, a slit of light signified another door. Sally knocked three times and the door opened. A large Italian with curly body hair around his neck opened the door. Sally walked underneath his outstretched arm. He tipped his cap to her. Sally held the Indian's hand and led her through the crowd.

The basement was windowless and stuffy, and the few electric bulbs created dark corners. They walked through the open basement that functioned as a restaurant with a few tables and a set of chairs. Miners sat waiting for the Chinese couple to make their meal in a makeshift kitchen the storeroom. Crowded gambling tables filled the back of the basement. An escape staircase next to the coalbin led to the street above should the police raid the joint.

Sophie Tucker's voice on the radio could not compete with the loud conversations. "Some of these Days" seemed melodramatic and somber around the laughing residents of Jerome. Sally scooted along the periphery of the room to the impromptu plank of wood that served as a bar. On the floor against the wall, opened crates held bottles of booze. Sally leaned on the wood and motioned two fingers to the bartender. A woman with swaying breasts and a pillowy face crossed over to them, annoyed. The Indian kept her head up but her eyes down.

"Hey, now, Sally. What you doing? I told you—you're still too young to be down here. I don't need customers thinking my niece is up for sale, you hear me, girl? Get home and take the Injun with you. She's ugly and will give the place a bad name."

Sally ignored her. "Oh, Aunt Bernice, fine, fine. We'll be gone in a minute."

Aunt Bernice smacked her on the side of the head and wagged her finger. "Stop drinking, too, while you're at it. What's Connie gonna think if she knew I let you drink? At least go back to the kitchen and wash some dishes to earn your keep."

Sally pretended to pout. "It's not my style to wash dishes. Besides, my mother must pay you something to cover costs. I'm guessing you make a bit of a profit having me here."

Sally pulled out a handful of change and two-dollar bills and released the money onto the bar. The Indian lifted her eyes to stare at the pile. Her lips moved, and then she spoke. "You made four dollars and sixty-seven cents tonight working as a dancer?"

Aunt Bernice shoved a man away who had grabbed her thick middle and attempted to kiss her. She turned toward the money. She grabbed the dollars and twirled her forefinger in the change. "Hey, now, Injun, how did you know there's four-sixty-seven in here?"

She pushed back her hair and studied the aunt. "My name is Kay."

Aunt Bernice burped.

Sally had been counting. "Wow! Okay, Kay. You were right. How did you count so fast?"

Aunt Bernice exploded with a laugh. Her mouth was a hole rimmed with drab teeth. "Whattaya know? A female Injun who can count."

Kay swore at her in German and called her a cow. "*Tante, du bist ein fette Kuh.*"

Sally said, "Let's go, Kay. I hear this shit every day."

Sally took one of the bills and put it in her front dress pocket as Aunt Bernice claimed the rest of the pile. She turned away from the girls and opened her arms to a man who gave her a big squeeze of a hug. Her laugh followed the girls back to the Italian who opened the door like a gentleman for Sally. She smiled and patted his arm. Once outside, Sally led Kay down the block to a two-story, brick boarding house with a side porch and several balconies. A horse whinnied in the windless night. The dry air was cold.

Sally led Kay up the backstairs to the roof. In the dark, Sally fumbled for the skeleton key hidden on the top ledge of the door frame and stepped carefully across the flat roof. Pointing up to the blazing Milky Way, she commented, "Isn't it something?"

Against the far wall, she inserted the long iron key into the keyhole and turned it to the right. Click. Sally pulled the door open, struck a match, and lit the kerosene lamp inside. Her bedroom was nothing more than a large utility closet, but she'd transformed the plain spot into a nest of privacy. After she had scrubbed the floors and swept out the ceiling cobwebs, she dragged up a rusty iron frame and mattress from one of the rooms below. She wedged a small chest of drawers at the end of the bed and pounded a nail on the opposite wall and hung a mirror. She turned on its side a wooden crate with Orange Nehi soda pop advertised on it. It operated as a table for the kerosene lamp and a tin can ashtray. Inside the crate, a large stack of magazines held it steady. Tonight, the lamp glowed. Sally motioned Kay into the room and closed the door. Cut and pasted on the walls were movie posters and the faces of stars. Sally watched Kay examine the glamorous poses of Marlene Dietrich and Louise Brooks, Buster Keaton and John Gilbert, Charlie Chaplin and Mary Pickford.

Sally turned her shoulder and lowered her eyes, mimicking the pose Kay touched on the wall. Sally asked, "Don't you think I look like Joan Crawford?"

Kay smiled. Her eyes jumped around the room that smelled faintly of lye. Sally sat at the head of her bed, took off her shoes, and leaned against the wall.

"Where'd you get all the pictures?"

"People leave magazines behind at the hotel, and I collect them."

Kay yawned and rubbed her temples. "*Ich muss schlafen.*"

Sally re-shifted her leg and held her knee. "It's late. Just sleep here tonight. There's room enough." She looked at Kay and studied her. "How could you know my Dad? What'd he look like, huh?"

Kay stretched her neck and looked at the movie stars smiling down at them. It didn't take long. She pointed to the blond actor with a thin mustache. "There. Your dad looks like him." Kay read the colorful movie poster aloud. "A Paramount picture, Zane Grey's *Wild Horse Mesa.* Starring Jack Holt, Noah Beery, and Douglas Fairbanks, Jr."

Sally laughed hard. She wore an outrageous expression as though she were still on stage and wanted the man in the back row to see her pretty white teeth. She grabbed a tin box which contained six rolled cigarettes.

She offered one to Kay, who declined. Sally tossed Kay her pillow and pointed to a wool blanket folded at the end of the bed. "You can sleep at that end." She turned the lamp flame low and laughed some more.

"If my dad were Young Doug! Ha! All my dreams would come true. He works for all the studios, you know."

Kay yawned and thanked her for the blanket. The lamp flickered around Sally's possessions and bounced shadows up the walls. Kay began her explanation.

"A tall man with one hand came to our farm around noon the other day. My guardian, Mr. Weese, had business to do with Mr. Vandenberg. The three of them met in the front yard. The tall man started yelling at your dad."

"Where were you when this was all going on?" Sally interrupted.

"I was in the field with the horses. I could hear them arguing. I walked to the house to see what was wrong."

Sally had an arm under her head. She looked up at the ceiling. "Go on."

"The one-handed man pushed your dad. Mr. Vandenberg took out a pistol and aimed it at him. That's when everyone got jumpy. The stranger pulled out his revolver and shot Mr. Weese instead."

Sally shook her head. "This is crazy. I don't believe you!"

Kay's words groaned. "I hid behind a tree and peeked through a bough. The tall stranger said your dad ruined the deal, and he'd have to fix his mistakes again. He shot your dad in the shoulder as a punishment."

"Oh, baloney!"

Kay's voice dropped and rumbled like thunder, "*Ich sah! Ich sah!*"

Sally sat up and wondered why she spoke German. Then she tried to imagine George Hero shooting her dad. She could imagine it easily. They had never liked each other, and George was hard-boiled. What did Connie Vandenberg want with the Weese farm? The German question paled in comparison.

Kay said, "The tall man could have killed your father. But he didn't."

Sally watched Kay's lips form her words slowly and simply. "I think he was sick. His face was puffy. He took out his handkerchief and wiped his gun with his one hand. Then he placed it in Mr. Weese's hand. He made it look like Mr. Weese shot Mr. Vandenberg in the shoulder."

Kay gathered her hair and braided a single side rope down the front of her chest. She whispered, "That tall man didn't see me. He wasn't counting on me watching the whole thing."

Kay stared at Bette Davis's platinum hair with finger-waves. Bette smiled at them with round eyes.

"What did you do?"

"The tall man said he'd go get a doctor. He told your dad to shut up and say nothing about the deal other than Mr. Weese tried to kill him and he shot back in self-defense."

What deal? Sally squeezed her eyes shut and tried to remember a conversation that involved the Weese farm, her aunt, her parents, and George Hero. She had been in Jerome for a year and learned to take anything Aunt Bernice said with a spoon of salt. Sally remembered reading a letter, or maybe it was a phone call from her mother, who raved about a vacation spot from the harsh Chicago winter. Connie had stayed at a Caribbean island on the Dutch side. She rambled on about a business venture. St. Maarten. Sally reckoned it made sense Aunt Bernice was getting her rum supply from somewhere. That she struck a deal with her sister to smuggle in rum from St. Maarten and store it at the Weese farm wasn't that far-fetched an idea.

Kay folded her arms. "I remember your dad. He came out to Clarkdale once before when Mrs. Weese was still alive. They wanted to own the property, not lease it. There was some kind of arrangement they were negotiating. Mr. Vandenberg came down from Chicago to sort it out. That was almost two years ago."

Kay sat with both feet firmly planted on the planked floor. "The tall man left in his white convertible. I could hear Mr. Vandenberg moaning."

Sally flinched but said nothing. Kay took a big breath and exhaled, and the kerosene light flickered. "I ran over to them. Mr. Weese was dead. Your dad was breathing hard. He was on his back looking up at the cottonwood trees. He told me to get the leather bag from his car. He told me you were up here in Jerome. He told me not to say anything to the police." Kay panted and mumbled, *"Er sagte mir, er liebt dich."* Then she switched back to English. Sally found it annoying.

Kay continued. "The contents in the bag are for you because he loves you." Kay wiped at her eyes. "He passed out and told me nothing more."

Sally listened to the words. Each sentence circled around her throat and squeezed.

"I did what he told me. I saw the bag in his car and grabbed it. I drove to the police and they carried your dad away to the infirmary in Clarkdale. They picked up Mr. Weese, and I suppose they'll bury him next to his wife at the Clarkdale Cemetery."

"You don't seem too sad about that."

"I had a room in the barn." She paused and said, *"Ich arbeite, das ist alles."*

There was a long pause. A time to digest all that Kay had said. Eventually, Kay concluded, "I hitched a ride from Clarkdale up to Jerome. It wasn't hard to find you."

Sally looked at Kay's glassy brown eyes. *Aunt Bernice was wrong.* Kay the Injun was homespun, but her eyes were observant, and it gave Kay an intelligent attractiveness. Sally admired Kay's perfectly shaped lips. She tried to ignore Kay's body odor. She believed Kay when she said she slept in the Weese barn and all she did was work. She was curious about Kay. Why the Deutsch? Sally remembered listening to the head housekeeper at the Pearson Hotel who spoke German. Sally understood some words of the language. Kay seemed fluent. How many years had she lived them? What about her real family? She imagined Kay as an orphan living in the barn with the other workhorses. Her Indian family had been slaughtered by white men, and the Weeses worked her like a slave and gave her a smack in the face if she spoke English. *Nur Deutsch!* That was the theory Sally was sticking with. She'd find out later how much she guessed was correct. She felt a pang of sympathy for Kay, as if her imaginings were fact. Kay didn't have to deliver Jonathan Vandenberg's goods to her. Kay could have run away. Sally admitted that's what she would have done. She was good at running away.

Her parents allowed her to stay in Jerome with Aunt Bernice. They checked in on her from time to time. That was it. She sighed sadly and felt a pang of pity for herself. Round and round the theories and questions about her family spun in her head, like a record playing a Wagner opera on the Victrola. She saw herself as the goddess of love, fertility, and beauty—Freyja, from *Das Rheingold.* She would endure the manipulations of her parents, escape from the giants, and protect the magic apples in her garden by following her dreams of stardom. Her grit would take her there. She was certain of it.

Kay reached down to the floor and grabbed a bag made of burlap. She pulled out Jonathan Vandenberg's possessions and gave Sally his leather notebook. It was stuffed with letters, lists, and several ten-dollar bills. Sally took the parcels, shoved them back in the sack, and threw it on the floor. She lay back and eyed the bundle. Kay frowned and took off her boots. She crawled under the blanket and moved her feet far away from Sally's face. They both said nothing. *One last cigarette.* Kay fell asleep quickly. Sally listened to her regular breathing and was surprised to find it calmed her. She refused to think about her father, but the sack with his possessions was a presence, a filler of space, and she let it fill the room with possibilities.

Sally remembered herself as a little girl at bedtime, when he played with her blonde braid, like the one Kay just made for herself. She remembered she had wrapped her arms around his neck and inhaled the sweet tonic he splashed on his cheeks after his shave. He would be leaving, she knew, and who knew when she'd have this intimacy again. A healthy dose of anger and panic consumed her. *Don't leave me with her!* She would have to keep her feelings inside. She would have to be quiet and watchful. Defensive. When Jonathan Vandenberg left on a business trip, she felt cold and hot at the same time. "Here, Sally," he gave her his pillow before he left, "hold this for me until I get back." It smelled of him, the sweet tonic mixed with his personal scent, and she clung to it at night. Throughout the early years of her childhood, it helped a little.

Then a few years later, after he was away most of the time in New York City, there was her sitter who filled the void. He was her father's childhood friend, a Negro to which Jonathan had felt an obligation. Jonathan watched over him, making sure he had a job at the hotel despite Connie's disapproval.

"Why do we need a mute, bow-legged man at my hotel?"

Casper's charm delighted Sally. His animated face drew her to him. She loved his ability to play the banjo and guitar. His tongue had been mutilated some time in his past. Though he mumbled to her at times, he preferred to express himself with an old banjo and a new guitar her father bought him for Christmas one year. Sally would listen for the rhythm and dance while absorbing his approval. Her mother called him the family pet. Sally thought she was mean to think of Casper like that. When Connie was busy or traveled, she allowed him to watch over Sally. He lit up Sally's life like going to the carnival at night, where the Ferris wheel never stopped spinning, and the ropes of white lights encircled her with a magical glow. However, Sally learned early that good feelings don't last for long. By the time George Hero came into the picture, Connie had removed Casper from the forefront of Sally's life and put him at the opposite end of the hotel, far below the seventh floor. He was ordered not to interact with Sally anymore. Sally disobeyed and visited him when she had the chance at the revolving front doors of the hotel when his shift started.

She rolled over a little and arched her back to look at the movie poster of *Wild Horse Mesa*. She waved the cherry end of her cigarette like a wand and traced the face of the son of Douglas Fairbanks. She started with the flip of his hair on his forehead, jumped to his serious light eyes, then followed his straight nose down to the pencil-thin mustache. *Jonathan Vandenberg*. He might as well be the son of Douglas Fairbanks. He was like a glossy, one-dimensional picture—completely inaccessible to her. She aimed the cherry and scorched a hole in his cheek. She instantly regretted ruining the poster.

"Shit."

Sally put out her cigarette in the tin can. She snuffed out the flame in the kerosene lamp. Blind in the dark, she opened and closed her eyes and stared drowsily at nothing. She tried to wrap her head around all that Kay had told her. A tall, one-handed man. A white car. Who else but George Hero? Sally cringed. She was fourteen when Connie Vandenberg hired him to be her patsy. In that half-asleep state where she could direct her thoughts and replay her past, Sally was not almost eighteen, but only fourteen when Connie summoned Sally to her suite, room 702, near the top of the hotel.

"George Hero, this is my daughter, Sally."

Sally noticed he was missing a hand and tried not to stare at the empty space below the cuff of his cheap shirt. He didn't say anything, only smiled down at her. The next time she saw him, he was slick inside a fine suit, and he smelled of spicy cinnamon and wood. It was obvious to Sally that Connie Vandenberg dressed him like a doll. He became her shadow, four or five steps away, lurking, standing against the wall as if he needed to hold it up or it would crash down on them. Sally's life had transformed into a distinct before and after. Before George, her parents were a pair, albeit a strained one, with little time and few smiles between them. Sally had Casper then. Sometimes he smuggled her to the Sunset Cafe in Bronzeville on the south side of Chicago to see the musicians play. She loved watching the black musicians and performers. It was where she learned how to do the Lindy Hop and heard jazz bands improvise. After George, trips to the Black and Tan nightclub ended. Casper's guardianship ended. Connie arranged for Sally's father to stay in New York City. He disappeared from regular view. Meanwhile, the man behind her mother kept silent but alert.

Sally avoided looking at him and pretended he was a statue, a coat of arms from Connie Vandenberg's room of antiques. She hated how he stood posed and stiff while his eyes followed a person around the room. When he did move, it was sudden. Sally detected a lightness, the faintest of smiles surfacing from George when guests flinched. The gesture was a reminder of his role as Connie's protector in a relationship that was possessive and constant. Sally stayed out of his reach, wishing she had time alone with her mother. Why did Connie need a bodyguard in the first place?

It was difficult to keep her distance all the time. Sally's room was connected to Connie's suite by a door. She heard them conspire with whispers. She heard the repetitive thudding of their bed at night and blocked her ears with her hands. When Connie wailed, Sally pressed her ears on their door and wondered if her mother was safe. One night, Sally thought for sure they were fighting. She heard a strangled, screeching sound, and she exploded into the room and yelled, "Stop!"

George sat on the side of the bed putting on his socks. Connie wore a towel wrapped around her waist. She pulled out a nightgown from the top drawer of her dresser. It was the maple drawer that sounded like someone being strangled.

George jumped and responded, "What?"

Her mother frowned and rolled her eyes. Sally slammed the door and ran back to her bed. The next day, while she was at school, workers had moved her clothes and tap shoes and dolls to the opposite end of the floor, room 722.

She resented George Hero's presence when Connie assigned him to pick Sally up after dance lessons or school. That had been Casper's job. There were two elevators in the lobby. She did her best to pick the one that had people in it. If only George and she entered the compartment, the ride up the elevator to the seventh floor was suffocating. She'd concentrate on the infinity of the mirrors that lined the interior. She studied George. To look at his reflection was not the same as to look at him directly, and the barrier gave her a sense of protection. His eyes looked funny. They were cobalt blue but brushed with a yellowish tint. He had dark circles under his eyes. He had smooth skin and high cheekbones. When Sally was older and had been to the movies several times with school friends, she had to admit George resembled Rudolph Valentino. It made her mad. How dare he look like a dreamboat and one of her favorite actors? It tainted her feelings for both men.

The more possessively her mother behaved toward George, the more repugnant he became to Sally. Connie went about her hobbies of buying and selling antiques and collecting precious stones. What financed her hobbies was overseeing the family-close corporation, the Pearson Hotel, at Water Tower Place. When Sally reached her seventeenth birthday, she dodged them both. She ran away to Jerome. Sally picked the copper mining town because she'd that read directors fancied Arizona for film locations, and the only relative who would take her lived there. Sally stole rolls of money from her mother's strangling maple drawer and hopped on a train. It arrived in Arizona two days later. Aunt Bernice displayed little affection for her rich sister in Chicago. She seemed pleased that Connie had failed as mother and allowed Sally to stay at her boardinghouse. Sally welcomed her new life. She would stay sharp and listen. She would refine her performance skills as a Copper Cutie. She would elbow her way into the movie business when an opportunity presented itself. If not in Arizona, then she would ride the rails to Hollywood and become a star. She was certain of it.

CHAPTER ONE

* * *

The next morning, Kay followed Sally around Jerome like a stray dog. Sally enjoyed watching Kay's wide-eyed expression as she took in the vitality of Jerome. Kay told her it was the first time she'd had a reason to come up to the mining town. Sally looked about with fresh eyes, remembering her first impression of Jerome had been raw and dirty and exciting. Kay commented she had never seen so many people shuffling about. The noise of their conversations and the black Model T cars chugging by made her feel, she told Sally, like an ant on a hill.

While they paused at the highest street to catch their breath and look around, Sally told Kay what she knew of Jerome. Carved into the side of Mingus Mountain, the hairpin road switched three times upward. Crammed on each side of the streets were merchant stores, saloons, and too few homes for 2,000 residents. Most were immigrant miners who worked in shifts for the United Verde Copper Company, owned by the family of William A. Clark. He was the famous copper baron and California senator with a fortune estimated at a half a billion dollars. His son, William A. Clark Jr., had dated Connie briefly in 1905 when he stayed in Chicago at the Pearson Hotel.

Sally conceded she liked the paintings of her mother when she was young. Connie had an enviable hourglass figure. Though Connie was considered a beauty, she had been criticized for her indelicate manners. Sally vaguely recalled a connection between Connie, Aunt Bernice, and "Billy," but she didn't know what it was all about and didn't care enough to ask. She knew better than to air the family's dirty laundry, but Sally couldn't stop talking.

Sally jabbered on, having found in Kay an audience who hung on her every word. "In Jerome, I have a place to stay and the freedom to dance and perform." She felt that Casper would approve. She told Kay about him. "Casper taught me how to listen to a Jazz band. Did

you know each instrument has a personality of its own? That each per-
former improvises to the other and each time they play a tune, it's
different? I like Jazz music. Do you?" Not waiting for an answer, she
told Kay about dancing on stage at the Sunset Cafe in Chicago with the
other performers who patted her head and called her the club mascot.
"Man, it was the best time of my life." Then she sighed heavily. "Now
Casper's a doorman at my mother's hotel. I don't think he performs
much anymore. I hope he's okay."

Sally took Kay to the second floor of the boarding house to the com-
munal bathroom and locked the door. She ran water in the porcelain
tub and added soap flakes until the bubbles jiggled. She assessed Kay's
shabby dress and matted hair and told her she stank.

"Even though Aunt Bernice says it's a waste of good water, I try to
bathe every day. You really must do it more often," she explained to Kay
as she helped her take off her clothes and examined her nakedness. Kay
blushed. Sally looked at her dispassionately as though Kay were a rag-
amuffin that had fallen into a mud puddle. Sally wanted to salvage her.

"I've got dresses in the costume closet. You soak, and I'll be back."

Though the tub was long, Kay's heels went up over the end and
exposed her callused feet. Sally left her to listen to the tub sprocket
drip water into the mound of bubbles. The water cooled. Sally burst
into the room with an armful of clothes and set them on a bench next
to the vanity cabinet. Kay stepped out of the gray water and dried
herself modestly behind the towel. Sally threw away the bandages
that functioned as Kay's brassiere and gave her a soft, side-lacing
bra and cotton panties. Kay put on the clothes Sally brought her. It
looked like a cowboy costume, and she looked at Sally with a confused expression as if Sally were playing a joke.

"Whattaya know, an Injun-Cowboy," Sally said, mimicking her aunt.

Kay ignored the remark. She shook her head and said, "This looks
ridiculous."

Kay took off the vest and chambray shirt. She put on a simple white blouse and left on the wide-legged gauchos, preferring them to her old dress. Sally nibbled on a piece of bread coated with butter and sugar. She tore it and gave Kay half, who devoured it.

Sally lifted a handful of Kay's wet hair and tried to smooth her locks with a brush. Sally inspected the ends. "Have you ever had your hair cut? Mind if I cut it?"

Kay's eyes bulged. "To your length? *Nein.*"

"No, it wouldn't look right at your ears. Let me trim up the ends a few inches. Your hair looks like the tail end of a horse."

Sally was glad Kay snickered and took that for consent to grab the black shears from the top drawer of the dresser. Sally chattered about the upcoming day while she observed Kay's facial expressions as she sat on the toilet seat looking at her new clothes. Sally's soft hands snipped the black straw that was Kay's hair. Sally thought of farm animals who twisted their heads to ponder why someone had laid hands on their flanks. They considered the gesture, their dumb eyes neither accepting nor rejecting the touch. This was how Kay looked at her now, blinking and holding her breath. Sally looked into Kay's eyes and saw her question, *Is this an act of pity or friendship?* Sally sensed her initial theory about Kay's lack of human interaction was correct. Kay had the countenance of a person who had been in the dark too long, only to be brought forward into the light and was uncertain whether to stretch in the warmth or bolt in fear of the unknown. A ray of sun stabbed into the high window and illuminated the drab bathroom. The water gurgled out of the tub, and Sally faced Kay with dancing eyes.

"Later on, we have to get dolled up and go to the Grand Hotel. Tonight's the first night of the Thursday night Knickle-hoppers Dance."

Kay did not understand her. Her eyebrows furrowed.

Sally's dark hair bounced below her ears. She did a Charleston step.

"Dancing. Men will come and pay for a dance. We'll make a nice pile of change, we will. You'll see. For now, let's go walk around town."

Kay asked, "What about Jonathan Vandenberg? Don't you want to see your father?"

"You told me he was in the infirmary in Clarkdale. Convalescing." Sally froze for a couple of seconds, and then inhaled sharply and arched her eyebrows as if struck by a great idea.

"Let's spend one of those ten-dollar bills he left me and buy a new hat and stockings. We could check out what new movie is playing at the Clarkdale Majestic. We could stop by and see your farm animals. Visit the graves of Mr. and Mrs. Weese. Whatever you want—if you agree to stay with me and dance tonight. I like you."

Sally took out a ten-dollar bill from her clutch and waved it in the air. "First, though, we need to eat, compliments of Mr. Jonathan Vandenberg." Her sleeveless dress was turquoise with a ribbon bowed at the hips. Black pleats fell to her knees. She put on a black straw cloche over her bobbed hair and dabbed red lipstick to her lower lip.

Kay followed her obediently. She waved her head and ran her fingers through her hair, which fell to her armpits instead of her waist. She put on the cowboy hat with a pinched brim that concealed her eyes. As they descended the stairs of Aunt Berenice's boarding house, Sally's shoes clacked, and Kay's boots thudded. Sally smiled. If she had said they were walking to California instead of around the corner, Kay would have followed her. She was certain of it.

They left the boarding house and trekked down the asymmetrical street that clung to the side of the mountain. The Verde Valley sprawled before them, a mile down and thirty miles wide. The blue sky was an inverted bowl. They passed several saloons, a bank, and a mercantile shop. Farther down the street was the tailor shop, a school, and houses on stilts that clung to the side of the road. Miners and proprietors engaged in conversation while ladies in dresses called for their children who ran circles around their skirts. A scantily clad woman hung out a window and called at a miner to pay for some attention. Burros carried mining supplies and packages. Carts with sweating horses competed with black Model Ts for space on the street. A whistle sounded below them in the distance. More whistles blew in reply, signifying a new shift was starting. Groups of miners appeared and disappeared at random. The air carried the smell of dung and smoke and sweat that oiled the doorways and wooden window frames. The cobbled road intersected a bend. At the end of a street, the switchback rose sharply upward. Sally pointed to the Montana Hotel, which sat at the top of the highest switchback. Sally agreed with Kay. To the heavens, they were ants scurrying about under the blue bowl.

A Chinese man stood on the porch of the English Tea Room. He bowed slightly when Sally and Kay entered. It was late morning, and there were few people sitting on round stools bolted to the pine floor.

"You can only find room in here between shifts." Sally informed Kay that there were three shifts at the UV Copper Mine. When the men worked in the mine, the town grew quiet. "It's the only time you can hear yourself think and get a bite to eat."

Mr. Yee seated them by the window and waited. Sally raised two fingers. "Pie and oolong tea, please."

He wore a black shirt, white pants, and a long apron. He mumbled in Chinese and turned away. A minute later, he brought back two plates of chop suey and two cups of water.

Sally put her elbows on the table and smiled. "Ask what you want, but he'll feed you only what he wants."

Kay gulped down her portion. Sally looked out the window across the street where the Jerome theater advertised the showing of *It*, starring Clara Bow. "I saw that show a couple days ago. Clara Bow. She's copying my hairstyle." She winked at Kay. Sally continued to stare out the window watching the people move up and down the street. She dropped her fork and gasped. "Damn if that isn't George Hero. Oh, rats, he has been sent to fetch me, no doubt."

Kay took her cup of water and poured it into her canteen. She insinuated with a nod of her head that she wanted Sally's water. Sally pushed the cup to her and crouched low in her seat. Kay looked out the window to where Sally pointed. Kay's eyes widened.

"That's the man who shot Mr. Vandenberg. Who is he?"

"George is my mother's everything fella. Officially, he's her guard and picks up the antiques she buys." She put some change on the table and bent low to leave the diner. Outside, she made a sharp left out of view and stood there putting her gloves back on. "My mother is an expert at collecting things. Antiques. Strange artifacts. Like George Hero." She straightened herself and touched her waist and hips, checking her posture in the reflection of Paul and Jerry's Saloon. A man with a potbelly and boiler hat kissed her through the window. She sniffed and the girls walked away.

"I don't know where she found him, but he's been around since I was close to fourteen. He gives me the creeps. A real killjoy."

Kay took a drink from her canteen and put it back in her burlap bag. She swung it over her shoulder and shortened her steps. They walked to an area where trucks and donkeys and Model Ts lined up next to each other. "What don't you like about him, Sally?"

"One minute he's right as rain. Then, those eyes of his have no soul. He's scary." Sally leaned forward and whispered, "I think he's bumped people off. For my Mom. Connie Vandenberg."

"What does your father think about George?"

Sally rolled her eyes. "When Connie and George start scheming, my dad vacates. You see, my mom inherited two hotels. One in Chicago and one in New York City. My father oversees the New York City hotel most of the time. My mother controls the Pearson. Connie lives in room 702, and George is at her beck and call from 701."

She shook her head as if George was the pall, the wet blanket cover-ing her mood. "Who knows what happened to him to make him so balled up?" Sally sighed, resigned he was a lost cause. She turned to look over her shoulder. "George Hero. I think we ditched him. Let's go shopping."

CHAPTER TWO

GEORGE HERO

1922

He reached for the hand that was not there. He longed to grab his thumb, trace the outline of his fingers, or scrape off a lengthy fingernail. In his mind, he made a fist and punched the face of the dead soldier with the feminine features. Out of the shadows the sun poured into the cabin car, and George Hero squinted at the window as the train pulled into the Berlin station. The information board clicked the date: March 12. 13:00. Steam escaped from the train with a *whoosh*, and the iron wheels ground to a halt. Dimly, it occurred to George that he had been roaming without forethought two years since his discharge. He was reluctant to return to his parents in Chicago because he had discovered many widowed women in France were attracted to him. With his pitiful command of French and their few words of English, it was easier to communicate with smiles and sympathetic fingers. Especially if she had children. They looked up at the stump at his right wrist, and their eyes filled with curiosity and pity. He wrapped the hot wound with clean bandages during the day and massaged the stretched, shiny skin at night.

The ghastly stitching on the end of his wrist mirrored his thoughts. His indignation boiled for the skittish private who had misfired. During his week-long stay in the army field hospital at St. Mihiel, George mocked him by calling him Private Cox, playing with his pun by imagining daily ways of amputating the private's genitalia. He chopped, burned, shot, squeezed, and sawed off his manhood. *What am I to do with one hand?*

George was transferred to Camp Hospital No.4 in Paris, which was converted from abandoned school buildings into a makeshift hospital with no running hot water. He convalesced with 400 other wounded soldiers, his loneliness as profound as the pain which emanated from his amputation. When he was released, George's anger intensified when he failed at buttoning his shirt or shaping a tie. When he pissed, he had to ask for help to button his pants. He switched to trousers with zippers with limited success. It was impossible to tie his bootlaces. George practiced writing with his left hand. If he wrote very small, he had more control over his penmanship. He had a nurse post a letter to his parents: *February 3, 1919. Dear Mom, I lost a hand, but I'm still alive. Healing in a Paris hospital. Will be home soon. Love, George.*

After his discharge from the 103rd Infantry, he impulsively changed his mind and sold off his return passage for one hundred francs and two vials of laudanum. Private Cox was dead, but George Hero's anger lingered. It spread to the French women who broke convention and touched him freely. At first, he enjoyed the abundant opportunities for sexual interplay. Their eyes widened over his good looks. They hovered over his clumsiness, appeased and stroked him. In George, they saw a replacement for their dead husbands, and he learned to compensate for the lack of a hand.

At twenty, his broad shoulders and plump lips gave him an older, sensual appearance. A pattern emerged as he made his way with a map south into the French countryside avoiding the empty trenches, the mounds of shell casements, the grotesque trees, and the rubble of destroyed buildings. He loitered in towns and seduced the widows. George noticed their clothes were once of good quality but had worn thin, and their homes mirrored the state of their clothes. Before the Great War, houses had colorful doors and whitewashed walls. Now, crooked shutters leaned to the ground, and fences faded to brittle gray. He would walk up and offer his services in exchange for food and a night's stay in the barn. On the first day, he was polite and completed chores he could manage with the help of her children holding a nail or gripping a tool. He surveyed the property, the windows, and the exit doors. He worked his way inside and ate at the kitchen table. Her stew was delicious, he praised, and the hand on hers, brief. On the second day, as she hung her clothes on the line behind the house, he tripped and pretended to fall. He grabbed her waist and held her. She blushed and patted his shoulder. That evening, he leaned forward after the meal and kissed both cheeks. She found brandy in the cupboard. He thanked her for bandaging his wrist which throbbed with pain. She sighed and expressed with her body how long it had been since a man had held her. They rolled on her lumpy mattress and slept. When they woke, his stump pulsated with a heartbeat of its own. He asked where he could find an opium den. In Lyon. In Saint-Étienne. In Avignon. He let the opium dens dictate his direction, and the widows became checkerboard pieces as he leaped from one to another.

One late fall outside Bourges, he met a young mother whose husband had propped a Sunbeam motorcycle up against the side of the house when his conscription orders told him to report to the town square in 1917. It still awaited his return. George figured he'd have to replace the crank and give the 3.5 horsepower engine a tuning. The back tire sagged. It was the first time since his amputation that his heart had lifted with excitement. Could he get parts? He worked on it with the help of

her eight-year-old son. They made a handsome pair, three hands manip-
ulating the machine, and it charmed the widow. She gave herself with a
passion that surprised him, and he stayed in her warmth while the snow
fell, and icicles spiked down off the fascia. 1921 came quietly. Winter's
pastel skies deepened as spring arrived and turned the earth spongy.

She followed him around the room with her eyes. She fussed with
his clothes and claimed his body parts with roving fingertips. When he
sat down, she leaned a hip on the arm of the chair, patted his crotch,
and waited expectantly for him to pull her into his arms. Her insatiable
need for affection annoyed him. George grew restless. He confiscated
her dead husband's wallet, a tie already formed into a knot, a jacket
that fit, and a pair of loafers a little too small, but at least he could slip
into them without needing help to tie the laces. The motorcycle rumbled to life and his departure came swiftly thereafter. He felt a twang
of guilt as he aimed for the Mediterranean. He imagined her returning
from her errand from the village. He heard her chirp his name with two
syllables as she checked the barn, the kitchen, and the cellar. He saw
her brace herself. Each time she called out "Geor-gee," her voice lowered into a whine. He imagined her eyes filling with tears when she saw
the motorcycle was gone. Perhaps, she would reason, he just went for
a trial run. She would hiccup with hope and dash upstairs to see if his
possessions were still in her bedroom. But nothing of him remained,
and her tears dripped off her chin. He could see her clearly as though
she sat on the handlebars.

George maneuvered around a sharp bend and the bike wobbled. He
drove slowly and focused on balancing. He had figured out a way to roll
cotton towels and secure them with a strap to his elbow so he could bal-
ance the right side of the handlebars. Gingerly, he braked with his left
hand and leaned as a counterweight. He would miss her smooth shoulders and the ripples of her rib cage, where his fingers had traced, and
she had giggled. Her son would frown, confused that George had left

without a word. The boy talked with a sissy squeal. George clenched his jaw. He felt suffocated by the pair's silent insistence that he stay.

At night, he dreamed of mortar fire and the strobe lights from shells that punctuated the darkness. The tanks rolled, and the screams resulting from each hit reverberated in his mind. Fashioned from the fog of an opium high, he began to have a recurring dream where details grew sharp and shadows seemed real. In his dream, he swam in the air away from the sounds of the war using the breaststroke. He kicked his feet, but he floated nowhere. Shadows raced ahead of him like ghostly vapor. Then, superimposed on the backdrop of the night, a bombast of fire lit up and revealed the face of Private Cox. George swore at him. His dream shifted. He ran through the trenches, stumbling over the bodies cluttering the ground, and jogging with the rats in a maze that never ended. He turned a corner and there was Private Cox. He stood in front of George with a bamboo pipe, breathing and exhaling seductively, his long lashes flickering, his mouth puckering. It disgusted George. He reached for his gun but both hands were gone. George stood helpless. Private Cox gave him a lascivious grin and laughed.

George would sit up in bed and hit his head with his palm and wish he could expel the sounds from his ears. The women would sit on their knees and coo French phrases. After a year, he grew bored with the predictability of them all. Sometimes his actions grew rough, and his voice exploded. Sometimes in bed, he forced them into strange positions. He shoved them away and then started to cry. He begged them for forgiveness. Their eyes softened, and their worry lines disappeared when they tried to hold him. Abruptly his feelings flipped. He found them in contempt for forgiving him and started yelling again. He learned it was dangerous to stay too long, but the widows made it so easy to stay. They found him jobs he could handle, introduced him to family members, and brought friends over to inspect him. They were spiders that shed their filaments over his body and tried to wrap him in a cocoon. He bought another vial of laudanum from the apothecary and told himself it was for his aching stump.

He spent the winter of 1921 in Marseille in an apartment overlooking the harbor with an older, sallow woman whose appetites initially matched his own. The realization that he needed opium more than he needed sex or companionship began to creep into the shadows of his mind. He abandoned the dying motorcycle and bought train fare. He headed toward the one city that gratified those who sought to feed their strange sexual proclivities and addictions. Berlin. When he pulled into the city on March 12, 1922, he arrived with a decent wardrobe, a silver pocket watch, and enough money to buy a second-class passage from Hamburg to the United States when he was ready. George stepped down onto the platform, and a part of him mourned. His home in Chicago might as well have been on the moon. *I'm sorry, Ma. I think I lost more than a hand.*

Where to go in Berlin? He picked the subway line *Zooligischer Garten* because he liked the sound of the name. It reminded him when, as a boy, he had begged his folks to take him to the Lincoln Park Zoo. His father gestured him away before leaving for work in the basement of the Pearson Hotel. As a public works laborer, he maintained the engines and the boilers that provided water and heat to over two hundred rooms of the luxury hotel. George's mother, though, succumbed to his begging and a sensation of victory filled George's chest. The two of them spent the day strolling around the zoo grounds in awe. George's memory was a patchwork of images. The chimpanzee's rubbery arms reaching from one branch to another. A tiger panting and looking at George as though he were the curiosity. Elephant ears flapping. Striped legs meandering. A stiff breeze off of Lake Michigan carried the animals' stench, and he felt coated by their odors.

As he entered the gates of the Berlin Zoo, an energetic March sun over-warmed the day. The breeze carried a whiff of dung into George's nose. It comforted him. He sat on a bench that faced the lion's pen. The tips of a copper mane preceded the beast as he emerged from behind a boulder. It stepped down a level and looked at him. Then it paced back and forth and twitched his tail. George tucked his suitcase by his leg and watched the zoo visitors walk by him.

When he first saw her standing at the other end of the fenced pen with her coat draped over her forearm, holding onto the wire fence that kept the cat confined, George thought there was nothing remarkable about her. She was simply the only woman in his vicinity. Her blouse did not ripple in the wind around full breasts. Her skirt did not cling to a small waist. She was neither tall nor short, neither thick nor thin. Her legs were not shapely, her outfit not stylish. She turned toward him, lost in thought, and he wondered why she was alone at the zoo. He walked over to her, his polished suitcase in hand, and they looked at the lion together. He tipped his hat and smiled at her.

"*Helfen Sie, bitte, Fraulein.*"

"*Ja?*"

George stammered. "A room to rent. *Zimmer. Ein zimmer zu mieten.*"

She scrutinized him boldly. She tilted her head and her eyes traced the horizontal line of his shoulders. The dimple on his chin. The small mole sitting on top of his cheekbone. He showed her coins from his pocket and gave her his very best smile.

He motioned eating. "*Essen mit mir.*"

She looked at his coins and her pink nails touched her stomach. She pointed to the east, and they left the zoo. They crossed the street into a residential area of five-storied apartment buildings. Two blocks later, on the corner was a cafe. She motioned with her head, and they went inside. She ordered them two plates of knackwurst and creamed kraut, brown mustard, and black bread. He had a *Berliner Weisse*. She had coffee. She ate with two hands, her fork in her left, her knife in her right. She spoke German as though he knew the language fluently.

Little did she know that he had graduated school from St. Sylvester in Logan Square in Chicago with some knowledge of Latin and German. The nuns had encouraged him to apply for college, but he had not felt proficient in either language or passionate about a subject matter to warrant college. His mother's badgering to make something of himself with more schooling brought about fits of suffocation. To escape the decision, he had enlisted in the war.

In the Berlin cafe, George watched her lips and recognized most words, but he was so rusty with Deutsch, he understood little. When she paused from eating, he watched her painted pink fingertips flick the air as she punctuated her sentences. During calmer moments, under her chin, a pink nail propped up her face. He leaned closer to her. He noticed her looking at his stump and smiled politely. He leaned back and hid his right arm under the tablecloth. How had he failed at the zoo to notice the reddish strands framing her face? The hazel eyes? Her arched eyebrows lifted as she talked to him, and he confessed over her monologue, "If a face was a song, yours would be a Cole Porter melody."

She stopped talking. She blinked at him and tapped her hand once on the white tablecloth. *"Ja. Kommt mit. Wie heissen Sie?"*

He understood that. "George Hero."

"Mitzi." She stood and yawned behind her hand, her expression feline. The *Oberkellner* approached and collected some of his coins. Mitzi slid her hand through the crook at George's elbow and locked herself to him. *"Kommt,* George Hero. *Wir müssen zum Babelsberg zugehen."*

"Anywhere you want, doll."

Down the steps to the train station, he let her lead, motioning her to reach into his jacket pocket for money to buy tickets. To where, he did not know. She refused to take her hand off his arm. They lit cigarettes together, she with her spare hand, he with his only hand, and they laughed. She whispered to him in German. Surely she knew he could not understand, but he nodded and smiled just the same. Fifteen miles south of Berlin, they got off at the *Babelsberg* stop and took a taxi.

She brought him to the entrance of UFA motion picture production company and explained that the director of the company was Erich Pommer. At least that is what George thought she said. She brought him to the back lot where at the entrance door, George admired a large poster of a man in a tux with black eyes walking atop the city like a predator. At the top of the movie poster in black letters was the title of the film: *Dr. Mabuse, der Spieler – Ein Bild der Zeit. Regie: Fritz Lang.*

George was curious. What role did Mitzi play in all this? Who was this director, Fritz Lang? He passed through a hallway. Into an airplane hangar he entered and froze. Mitzi gently pushed him forward and escorted him down a series of set designs bordered by lamps clamped to cranes. A group of costumed actors stood on a cobble-stoned, slanted street. A tall man wearing a light blue suit and a monocle shouted through a megaphone at an actress in a fur coat and flimsy shoes. She covered her mouth with the back of her hand and ran off the set in tears.

Mitzi murmured her disapproval. George wondered if it was for the harsh director or the thin-skinned actress. The man with the monocle handed off his megaphone to an assistant and lit a cigar. He saw Mitzi and marched over to her. Mitzi shouted, "Fritz!" and offered up George like a rare find at a thrift shop. The director took Mitzi's hand and kissed it. He looked at George and circled him. Mitzi darted away, her hair bobbing. She brought back a man with bespectacled, sunken eyes and a wooden clipboard and pleaded, "Dean, *bitte,*" like a schoolgirl. He looked at George disinterestedly.

"*Guten Tag.* You're an American soldier? War's been over for two years, you know."

George sighed with relief. "Where you from?"

"Detroit."

"Chicago."

Dean extended a hand to shake, saw the stump and lit George a cigarette instead and handed it to him. "Where'd you find Mitzi?"

"I think she found me. At the zoo."

He smiled. "You saved her ass. Mr. Lang would have fired her today if she hadn't come back with a proper-looking German for his next scene."

"I don't get it. I'm not an actor."

"It doesn't take talent to look handsome standing in a corner at a party. The next few scenes we're filming require interior shots of a casino. You just have to pretend you're gambling."

Dean examined the sheet of paper on his clipboard. With a gangly finger, he pointed George to the interior set of a room with black booths surrounding a huge circle. White tracks meant for placing bets sloped downward to where the Boxman would collect the bet. Workers adjusted levers that allowed the platform to rise and disappear out of view.

"Mitzi found you at the zoo during the day in the middle of a workweek with that suitcase. Are you coming or going?" Dean erased something from his ledger and set it next to his hip. "My guess is you don't have much going." He pushed his round glasses up on his nose and waited for George to respond. George said nothing.

"Listen. I can have a contract drawn up in an hour. You'll be paid as an extra. Maybe you'll rise to bit part." Dean added sarcastically, "Who knows, if Fritz Lang likes you, you might get a part in his next film and become a star."

George looked around the hangar at the commotion of cast and crew. He noticed the swearing and laughter. Sweating workers toiled under the harsh stage lighting. Bored faces stood in shadows. Asymmetrical set pieces held macabre props and gave George the feeling he'd walked into a nightmare. Mitzi returned to them, smiling. George wanted to grab her around the waist and smell her.

Instead, he asked Dean, "Why are you here? What's your story?"

Dean tapped his ledger impatiently. "I came over a couple years ago after the war ended to visit my grandparents. Mitzi found me, too.

They like me here because I speak both English and German."

George hid his stump behind his back and scratched his neck with his left hand. "I don't need to be famous. How much?"

"Not much. Your name?"

"George Hero."

Dean tilted his head and his glasses slipped to the end of his long nose. He stared at George. "It's bedlam, you should know. Lang's a perfectionist. He will work you long hours from the afternoon until the middle of the night. Sometimes, you'll feel like pulling out your hair. But his wife, Thea, will feed you. And there's a room you can stay in next door to the studio. We have a whole floor of rooms set up for extras and technicians. You'll be bunking with a couple other guys."

Dean strode away telling George over his shoulder to wait there while he went to get a contract. George turned in a slow circle. Mr. Lang demanded quiet and filming resumed. Male and female characters in tuxes and shimmering gowns with caked-on makeup and exaggerated eyeliner sat around a circular table with their hands outstretched. Their thumbs and pinkies connected and created the shape of the sun on the table. Positioned overhead was a man kneeling on a rafter with his film canister between his legs, cranking the lever and catching the dramatic image of the hands on the table below him. George strolled away.

A pair of workers prepared a set by painting arabesque swirls on the make-believe walls of a lobby. Another technician climbed a ladder and replaced the bulb in the spotlight erected at the edge of the set. George watched a horse being led down a cobbled passageway. Painted plywood cut like heavy arches framed the alley. Sleepy dark houses with silent draped windows gave the impression it was after midnight. The horse turned a corner out of view. George wandered after the echo of its hooves clipping the road. A different set faced him, the inner chamber of a house, a private parlor. The walls were papered in gilded stripes. Harlequin-patterned shutters framed a cabinet with lizard knobs. Geometric patterns of the room exuded elegance and mystery. A grand piano stood in the corner. Poised on the set was an actress in costume. She wore a strange black gown with white silk pockets sewn around her slim hips and pearls hanging like a rope around her neck down to her knees. She stepped off the set and left it empty. George blinked several times. *What a bizarre world.*

Dean's irked voice startled him from behind. "So, you found one of the sets we'll be using tomorrow. Great. Today, though, it's the casino. Go get fitted for a tux." He tilted the wooden clipboard to George and pointed his pen at him. "Sign this, and I'll take you to the seamstress."

What kind of movie was Fritz Lang making? Suddenly, a mental picture of Sister Maria popped in George's mind. He was a boy sitting in the front row at school. She wagged her finger at the class and quoted a pithy from George Washington: "It is far better to be alone than in bad company." He felt Sister Maria would not approve of the eccentric Fritz Lang or his clandestine film. George snickered. The premonition that the UFA movie studio would bring out the worst in him was strong in spite of the gravitational pull to sign up with this circus. Wasn't this the reason he came to Berlin in the first place? To experience the strange and feel the extreme? He felt the taste of opium in the back of his throat and longed for a hit. He thought of Private Cox who still haunted him in his sleep. In this weird place, George reasoned, he could kill off Private Cox for good. Kill the Great War from his mind. This new bizarre world of Fritz Lang could supplant the memories of the previous one. Wean him from the greater pain.

George muttered, "This crossroad will save me or kill me." With tiny strokes of his left hand, he signed his name on the contract.

* * *

Among the noise surrounding George, he heard the commanding pounce on a piano. George followed the music and stepped up on the set of the geometric parlor. George faced the back of a woman with a bun, seated at the bench. She stressed a distinctive, slow march. Each chord was punctuated with an obscenity jumbled in French, German, and English.

"Schei-sse, Pu-tain, Ca-sse, toi, I-hate-you-hus-band, yes-I-do."

Behind her, George smiled at her trilingual profanity and stepped closer to see what she was playing. There was no sheet music. The heavy chords resonated like the plodding of a giant's footsteps. The pace quickened, then became furious. Her fingers rumbled down the keyboard, spreading wide in an outpouring of anger that made the piano roar. People paused as they walked by and then moved on as if her release was typical. George stood hypnotized. Her fingers rippled the notes until her hands cramped and she stumbled. She tried the passage again, slower. Her fingers would not cooperate.

She barked at the keyboard, *"Unmöglich!"*

She reset the pins in her bun and saw George grinning at her. She faced him with wild eyes and extended her hand. He kissed a knuckle. *"Ausgezeichnet!* You're amazing."

She responded in English with a thick accent. "Rachmaninov. He and his 'Prelude in C sharp minor' can go to hell. With Fritz."

She stood. She was almost as tall as George. "I have to prepare the crew's supper. Do I know you?"

He tapped his forefinger to his eyebrow and saluted. "George Hero. I've signed up to be an extra in *Dr. Mabuse: der Spieler.*"

"Thea von Harbou. I wrote the screenplay." Her look was sharp. She stepped off the set and advised to George, "Run for the hills, Sheik."

Mitzi appeared, spotted George, and sighed with relief. She stood next to him, and they watched Fritz Lang's wife walk away. Mitzi folded her hands in front of her. He was hungry and charged with energy. He pulled on a lock of red hair next to her chin. When Mitzi smiled up at him, he pounced on her mouth and kissed her. When he released her, she bobbled backward. He stepped aside laughing, and she stood there with raised eyebrows, her hands still folded in front of her, blushing. George repeated the name of the seamstress Dean told him to see. Mitzi held his hand and led him to his fitting.

* * *

Sunken clouds spat a late April rain on the back of George's neck. He entered a cracked lane overtaken by weeds toward an abandoned water tower of chocolate bricks and curved windows that looked like drowsy eyes. The architecture was nothing like the white water tower in Chicago where as a boy he had watched his father work as a foreman. This one was a rectangular box eight stories tall, a fortress from a medieval dream. As George approached the back door, the bumpy clouds obscured the morning light and gave the building a sinister appearance. The dampness absorbed into the stump at his wrist, and it ached as he poked at his neck trying to stifle the itch under his skin. It had been three days since his last visit to Mr. Li's opium den.

Within walking distance of the UFA studio complex, hidden from the main road behind vines that coiled around the Hemlock trees, he knocked on a door and waited for a Chinaman to open the center window and admit him. The small window-door snapped open, and a man with puffy eyes squinted at him. He recognized George and let him in. George hunched down and followed, watching his braid roll on the back of his tunic as he led him through the basement. Room dividers partitioned a corner, and as George whiffed the aroma of opium, he salivated. A pot-bellied stove heated pots of water and warmed the area while a young worker prepared gallons of opium tea. Kerosene lamps sat on tables and a davenport. George walked over to the old man who organized the den and gave him Deutschmarks.

"*Guten Tag*, Joe," he greeted George with snipped syllables. "Here." He patted one of eight army cots, each covered with a military blanket, all positioned in a circle with a center island for the young worker on a stool. His worktable contained candles, matches, bowls, opium pods, a pestle and grinder, tubes, bamboo pipes, and a hookah. He had a long, curved pinky nail which was filed and used as a spoon.

"Hello, Mr. Li."

He kicked off his soggy loafers and placed them next to the stove to dry. He set his overcoat on a wooden chair by his cot and lay down feeling like a bug on an ashen petal connected to a dead daisy. As he waited for the opium to foam so he could inhale the vapor, he ignored the other bug two cots away and stared at the room divider. There was a red dragon coiled and twisted on a silk panel. He inhaled and closed his eyes. Soon the flush dulled his senses. That dullness turned into a stupor like a blanket that covered him with nothingness, and he floated to a place where Private Cox could not penetrate. In this dreamy blackness, his one impression was that he was in his mother's womb, and his relief became an audible groan. He lay there for several hours before he had to report for filming.

* * *

When George was not at the studio or the den, he was with Mitzi at her apartment, charming her to let him sleep on the couch rather than sharing a room with a smelly carpenter and the prop master's assistant. George had attempted to share her bed, but she refused, and he thought it oddly refreshing that element was excluded from their time together.

Instead of sex, they cooked. This was a new discovery for George since Mitzi insisted he pitch in and help with his one hand. Mitzi liked to bake first. Alternating between rising dough and preparing a dessert, the apartment warmed with the smell of bread baking and strudel filled with apples or chocolate pie. Most times she made too much. She gave the surplus to the cast and crew who eagerly devoured her leftovers.

George watched her pink fingertips--she never changed colors--follow the directions from a recipe card pulled from a box with *Mitzi's Schatztruhe* hand painted on the lid. With Mitzi as a mentor, their three hands created flavorful meals like plum sauce for pork loin or pan frying the breaded veal bought at the butcher. She peeled and he chopped the vegetables. They seasoned soups and baked stews with dumplings. They chose to share a large plate using two forks. They leaned in and touched foreheads and exclaimed, *"Prost!"* They slurped up noodles and wiped their plates clean with her warm bread. She served him cool milk. George agreed her box of recipes was indeed a treasure chest filling more than their empty stomachs. Cleaning up could wait an hour. They lit a cigarette and sat on the couch to digest the food, and then the talking would begin.

His Deutsch was slowly getting better, and he shared English words when she asked. She liked to talk quickly, her hair swinging under her chin, brown lashes lifting her eyes, and he listened to her chatter, understanding half of what she said. He brought with him Mr. Li's tea in a quart jar. It was pungent and potent and kept him in a semi-state of drowsiness. George felt like his days were reversed from normalcy. They took the train to Babelsberg and reported to the UFA studio at two o'clock in the afternoon. Mitzi went to meetings with the production staff while George stood around and waited for instructions as an extra. After the first month, he found the filming with Fritz Lang to be as tiresome as Dean had warned. Fritz swaggered around each scene and projected orders through his megaphone. Groups were corralled, waiting for his command to move en masse. Whether filming the principal actors or engaging a group, take after take, Fritz Lang was the potter who shaped and molded the actors to his will. Only Thea Von Harbou barked back at him, or made suggestions where to aim the camera to Carl Hoffmann, or explained her ideas of the set designs to Otto Hunte and his team. George admired her for standing up to her husband. Thea challenged Lang's intellect. She had ideas and reminded him that she had written the script.

George also understood Fritz's attraction for the pretty girls surrounding him. They stroked his ego and undermined Thea's femininity. The more Thea pushed, the more Fritz engaged his body with petite, demure women who idolized him. Day after day, George stood in the shadows and watched the two spar. He hid jars of Mr. Li's tea in strategic places, smoked cigarettes, and stood like a mannequin when directed on the set. He ignored his tight collar, his slicked hair, the sweat dripping inside his suit as lamps heated his powdered face and caused the black eyeliner to drip. Meanwhile, Carl Hoffmann cranked the film into metal canisters on stilts. The pattern continued until George felt like a set piece within a snow globe. Despite the commotion, despite the effects of Mr. Li's tea, George felt the beginnings of a restlessness similar to what he had experienced with too many women in France.

George liked the congenial side of Thea's personality. Six days a week, she served soup or sandwiches promptly at 2100, with a wide smile showcasing straight teeth and magenta lipstick. It was her way of thanking everyone for seeing her vision of the film into fruition. Thea accepted Mitzi's breads and desserts warmly and accepted thanks for the meal from the cast and crew. Afterwards, the filming continued until two in the morning. Back at Mitzi's apartment, George and Mitzi sipped Peppermint Schnapps, and he listened to her unload her impressions of the day's filming before she retired to her bedroom and he reclined on her couch. He suspected his inability to understand her fully provided a certain freedom for her to say whatever came to her mind. It seemed to them both that their perfunctory replies to the other during the day led to a backlog of words wanting release. When alone, he started to tell her his thoughts in English. After the jerkiness of many hours translating in his head and spitting something out in German hoping it was correct, it felt great to speak English unadulterated, whether or not Mitzi understood.

She seemed to understand his need to share his past and refrained from talking when it was his turn. He told her about his childhood and his parents, about his neighborhood in Logan Park, and his schooling. He paused when he came to a section in his narrative that was particularly embarrassing. She looked at him with eyes that did not judge. Secrets were safe. After he revealed the general parts of his childhood, one night he tested Mitzi with a horrific incident.

"So, I guess I was around thirteen," he began. "I was working with my dad in the Pearson Hotel boiler room. There were six mechanics fixing things, maintaining the valves and pipes. They didn't like the new guy, Cicero, who had recently installed a new elevator system at the Drake Hotel. Someone hired him to be in charge of putting one in for us at our hotel." George made a smacking sound with his cheek. "It didn't go so well for Cicero."

George peeked at Mitzi who sat on the opposite side of the couch filing her nails, her legs stretched and crossed at the ankles. The light from the table lamp made her calves glow. She watched his face without a reaction. He puffed on his cigarette and continued.

"He was a Pollack from a neighborhood called Cicero. He was short and had polio, so one of his legs was thinner than the other, and he wore a brace and limped. He'd smack the floor with his shorter foot. It annoyed everyone when he walked on the cement floor of the basement. The guys would walk fast down the corridors just to harass him. To see him huff to keep up. And Cicero still kept bossing everyone around like he was some hotshot. He had shifts going around the clock, hurrying to get that elevator working. Everyone was beat. One day on my old man's shift, before sunrise, the gang was installing the pipes in the elevator shaft. Cicero said something condescending. The men were fed up. They started pushing him around. They made a circle and they all started insulting Cicero and shoving him across the circle like some ball at school recess."

George sighed and took a drag. Mitzi stared at him with inscrutable eyes. He pressed his lips and looked into his cup of tea propped on his thigh.

"I don't know, Mitzi. I stood there and watched them beat the shit out Cicero. Literally. They cracked his skull with a pipe wrench. The blood stained the floor." George lowered his voice and whispered to his cigarette, "Like some game, they jumped around and dodged the brains, the blood, and the shit. I stood there watching them do this. I just stood there." George stamped out his cigarette in the ashtray. He stared at the wall.

"My dad. He saw me. He handed me the pipe and said, "Hey, son. Wanna take a swing?" George closed his eyes. "Someone opened up the boiler door. They were talking about getting rid of his body. One of the bastards found a ratchet saw for cutting pipe, you understand?"

George turned to Mitzi. His throat warbled, "I ran out of there as fast as I could. No one said anything. Cicero just disappeared. They hired someone else. He was tall. Quiet. And the elevator works just fine at the Pearson Hotel."

George gulped down his tea. "That night I understood something about us all. Nothing better than scavengers. Jackals. That's what we are. Those men for doing it. And me. What am I? I did nothing."

They were silent. Through Mitzi's apartment window, the rising sun pierced a smooth ray through the blackness of the night. From the couch, George studied how the dawn transformed the face of the building across the street. At the right second, dozens of windows reflected the sun and turned into shiny squares. He faced Mitzi. She blinked at him, and he wondered how much she understood. He waited for her to reach over and hug him and say everything would be okay, that after all he was just a kid, that he wasn't at fault. But she didn't. He was glad for that.

* * *

The filming continued into June. The film crew, the production crew, and principal cast met in the large front office of UFA, and they wait-ed for the producer Erich Pommer to arrive and conduct the meeting. George stood a few feet away from those assembled in his usual spot against the wall, sipping his spiked tea despite being neither a princi-pal cast member, a set builder, nor a filmmaker. However, he had been watching Carl Hoffmann set up the cameras. George was close at hand, and he became a gopher. Under Hoffmann's direction, George helped organize the reels. He enjoyed watching the editing team snip and glue the film strips together to create the whole story. When he had nothing to do but wait for the next set of instructions, he observed. He stood still, back against the wall, silent. Thea teased he looked like some ob-scure soldier standing at attention. She ran her finger across his straight shoulders and leaned in suggestively to be kissed. George turned his head and refused to do so.

Dean talked, and Mitzi took notes. He told Fritz he finally found the perfect woman to rise up out of the floor during the gambling scene, a table-lady called *Die Nordische Königin* at the Kakadu Bar, a popu-lar cabaret on *Joachimslater Strasse*. Fritz wasn't listening. He inched up behind Mitzi and whispered in her ear while his hand patted her rear. George opened his mouth to protest but Mitzi pushed Fritz's hand away and stepped out of reach. She gravitated toward Thea and jotted something down on her paper tablet. Thea rolled her eyes. To George, Thea announced loudly in German, "If we are all going to the Kakadu

Bar, you must join us, Sheik. I insist. I need a dance partner, and Fritz is too busy to be a husband."

That was two days ago. George would go because he would sit at the best table in a swank nightclub in the western side of Berlin. He would go because he wanted to see something other than the film studio. In the last three months, he went from being semi-included in conversations to a must-have at parties. He had grown closer to Thea and Fritz. He was friendly with Dean and the rest of the cast. Still, he counted the days to when they'd wrap up the shooting, and he would be free from his contract. He had saved enough money to buy his return passage from Hamburg to Chicago. He considered asking Mitzi to join him.

It was she who had recently initiated their consummation. She had come out of the bedroom in a robe and stood at the end of the couch where his feet hung off the end. She grabbed his big toe and squeezed. He awoke and watched the robe fall from her shoulders, and then she climbed on top of him with a mixture of coquettishness and trepidation, dipping her shoulders as she crawled over his skin, her shiny pink nails holding his shoulders down, blushing all the while, and his feelings for her cut through the fog of sedation. Mitzi's sincerity felt profound compared to the dreamy expressions in the odd world of the film. They slept. They clutched. They slept some more. Dean called her on the telephone and yelled at her for going AWOL. Then he changed his tune and told her Fritz and Thea would pick them both up in the convertible in an hour.

They crammed into Fritz's Mercedes 28/95 sport with Carl Hoffmann behind the wheel and Fritz next to him. Dean, Mitzi, George, and Thea stuffed themselves in the back seat. George lifted Mitzi to his lap before Thea had a say about the seating arrangement. They drove down the boulevard of *Kurfürstendamm* to the Kakadu Bar. They were ushered through the main doors into the brightly lit club. Between walls fashioned in white stripes, they moved past potted palms and gold velvet seats surrounding small tables. Red stage lights gave a lush tint to the velvet drapes framing the polished wooden bar. They walked past it to the private rooms at the rear of the club.

"In fact, I should take you to North Berlin sometime. It's not as touristy as this district. When Thea sends me out for provisions, I go to the saltier clubs like The Karls-Lounge or take a stroll *unter den Linden* on *Friedrichstrasse.* What a crowd—the peep shows and doll-boys waiting to score."

They paid for a back room, ordered champagne and canapes, and squeezed into a booth. George sat at the edge and stretched out his legs. Thea sat on the other side and stretched out hers. Fritz sat in the middle and asked the waiter for the Butterfly Queen, who swirled on a side stage close to their table, wearing nothing but an elaborate headdress of feathers and a shimmering, sheer robe. The extensions sewn into the arms allowed her to lift and close the garment like a giant butterfly flapping her wings. When her routine was over, she exited the stage. A few minutes later, she was quite the sight, sashaying to the table wearing the butterfly robe, her breasts moving synchronously to the side-shifting of her hips. Her expression was one of disdain emphasized by the downward frown of her magenta lips. She struck a pose at the booth and inhaled the smoke from her cigarette set in a white holder.

Fritz Lang reached across the table to kiss her hand, but she was unimpressed. She pointed to Dean and said in German to Fritz, "He was here the other night and told me you had ideas of hiring me. Well, I'm not cheap. What kind of picture are you making?"

Unperturbed, Fritz repositioned his monocle on the top of his cheek. "My dear, you will do exactly what you are doing now, but imagine rising out of the floor in splendor. The scene is the interior of a high-class gambling house. All those who place their bets will be impressed by your beauty. Your body, my dear, was meant to be seen."

She scrutinized everyone at the table. She blinked at George and smiled. To Fritz she asked, "When and how much?"

"Tomorrow for two hundred."

"Five hundred. Deutschmarks don't buy much these days."

Fritz Lang laughed. "Of course. Your name, my queen?"

"Vera Lutz."

Fritz turned to Dean. "Arrange to have Vera picked up Tuesday and brought to the studio.

"Yes, boss."

Thea stood up. *"Lass uns Tanzen und Trinken."*

Fritz and Carl Hoffmann talked about how to shoot Vera on Tuesday. Mitzi sipped her glass of champagne and chatted with Dean. George's head throbbed. He wanted fresh air. Thea linked arms and led him out back to the alleyway. Down the long lane, the row of nightclubs had tables and chairs set in the semi-darkness. Couples blended into the shadows. Thea lifted her skirt. Around her thigh was a black band with loops that held a small spoon, folded cigarette paper, and a vial of white powder. She scooped out some of the powder to the paper.

"Here, George. Try this."

* * *

Thea's dress had layers of fringe that wiggled and made him dizzy. He concentrated on the pearls around her neck that hung like a rope down between her sizable breasts. She spoke to him, but her words were muffled, as though he were underwater. His eyes broke away from her string of pearls and jumped to the string of lightbulbs strung down the alley. Someone opened a door and music rumbled into the narrow lane. George recognized a Bessie Smith tune. Thea was saying something about the foreign minister Walther Rathenau and how horrible it was he had been assassinated. She lifted her glass of champagne and saluted Rathenau. George cringed as he watched her face turn green. *What had she added to the cocaine?*

He was no longer on a street corner. George was surprised to discover that Thea sat next to him in a taxi. The windows were rolled down, and George heard the sound of tires rolling on wet pavement. He felt the spray of rain on his cheek. Thea took out another white cigarette paper. She filled a layer of powder with her little spoon from the band around her thigh. George followed Thea's lead and snorted the contents. He slumped against his door window and watched the string of streetlamps pass him by until they had left the city, and the blackness of night cloaked everything. He was glad Thea's voice was muffled and he could not discern her political rant.

He was no longer in the taxi. He had awakened at Fritz and Thea's home in the affluent neighborhood of Babelsberg, south of Berlin in the Potsdam district. Their estate sat on the bank of the *Griebnitzsee* and was well spaced from their neighbors. Thea pulled him into the house and up the grand staircase to the second floor, where music played on the Victrola. Candles lit a room full of people laughing and talking in a cloud of cigarette smoke. In the center was a massive round coffee table. People played strip poker and a man stood up, having won the pot and stripped off his boxer shorts. The topless woman next to him was about to pay her dues. Thea turned to George and kissed him on the mouth. She took off his jacket and held his hand and led him into the circle of bodies. It added to his delirium. He crossed the sea of arms and hands and held the wall while the rip current pulled at him. Again, he heard Bessie Smith sing. He tried to listen to the lyrics of "Downhearted Blues" and focus on the string of notes to keep the panic from building in his chest. He swallowed back the reflex to vomit. His stood with his back to the wall facing the door to the room. It opened and Fritz and Mitzi entered. George squinted with disbelief. He panted with shock when Private Cox followed Mitzi into the room. Mitzi staggered in. Her blouse was ripped.

Amid the room of laughter, Mitzi looked at George with sad eyes, and he leaned toward her. Time vacillated between breakneck speed and slow motion that coincided with his heartbeat. Everywhere he looked, Private Cox had moved to stare at George with that ridiculous smile. Thea shouted she wanted to play Russian Roulette.

Sloppily, she held up a gold-plated pistol. "Compliments of Herr Goebbels, my new friend. He envisions a future of the restored glory of the Fatherland. He wants me to write screenplays. I think it's a great idea, but Fritz is not interested." She spun, looking around the room. "Where did he go?"

People were on their knees around the table waiting for Thea to begin the game. George reached for Mitzi. She stood by the door, covering her face, crying. Her painted fingernails were shiny and tapered. George concentrated on them as he staggered over to her. Private Cox had his arm around her shoulders possessively.

Thea's mood changed. She started yelling, swinging the gun around, "Everyone out! I've had enough of this party. Go home! All of you." People started to dress and creep out of the room. Bessie Smith stopped singing.

Through the fog of smoke, it grew quiet. The candles flickered. Fritz came out of the bathroom with a young girl whose eyes widened upon seeing Thea wielding the gold-plated pistol. The blonde squeaked and ran out of the room. Fritz frowned at Thea. He opened the window and fanned the room.

"Woman, what a racket you're making. You're an embarrassment. Put that gun down."

Thea waved the gold-plated pistol at Mitzi like a brandishing finger. "So, you want my husband *and* the Sheik. You aren't even much to look at."

George reached for the gun and grabbed her wrist. It went off. Mitzi gasped and grunted. She dropped to the floor. In his hand was the gold-plated pistol. All he could hear was Mitzi whispering his name. George collapsed next to her. Her eyes rolled. She exhaled loudly, and her eyes soon froze into hazel marbles.

George crawled backward. His one hand pushed the pistol at his temple while the room turned. Dean pulled him up.

Fritz ordered Dean angrily, "Get him out of here before the cops arrive and take that gun with you."

He turned to his wife and scowled. "What do you plan to do with her?"

Thea sat down in a club chair and lit a cigarette with shaky hands. "Let me think a moment." She closed her eyes.

CHAPTER THREE

KAY

1928

A pair of ravens soared in lazy circles high above the truck. Over Jerome, the empty sky and thin air felt heavy in Kay's ears. She returned her gaze to Sally, who was negotiating with a man for a ride down the mountain. She didn't want to waste her money on a taxi.

"Please, mister. Whattaya say? Just a ride down to Clarkdale is all I'm asking. My friend and I." He looked at Kay and opened the door to his Ford.

"You ride up here. The Indian can sit in the back."

Kay watched Sally pull out a folded Chinese fan and snap it open it with a dramatic flip of her wrist. She fanned her face, vigorously combatting the moisture that pooled in drops on her upper lip. She smiled at Kay, pleased with herself for getting the free ride. She swirled into the front seat and leaned as close to the door as she could. Kay spit and climbed up in the back of the truck, sandwiching herself between two older calves. She guessed they were about eight months old, large enough to be pulled from their mother. The calves bellowed, and Kay rubbed their ears as she spoke German to them. There was a metal pan discarded with other rubbish in the truck bed, and Kay offered the calves a drink by pouring water from her canteen. She leaned against the one next to her, comforted by his wiry hair and noisy breathing. She recalled Sally's criticism that she stank and rubbed at the sweat on her forehead with the back of her hand. She thought about her deceased caregiver, the submissive Mrs. Weese.

Mrs. Weese was a quiet woman, but when she did speak, it was in German. She was mopish yet obedient to the wishes of her husband. She taught Kay how to scrub away the dirt from in and outside of the house. Kay learned her way around a German kitchen, including how to stuff the pork casings with sausage. Mrs. Weese taught Kay how to pick the vegetables from the garden and the fruit from the orchard. They canned their harvests in mason jars and set them in rows on wooden shelves built in the dirt cellar below the house. At the end of a day's work, she taught Kay how to change without exposing herself. *Nacktheit ist eine Sünde.* Kay alternated between three smocks and a nightgown, ever mindful to hide her body because nakedness was a sin. The bathroom in the house was so tiny that when Kay's growth spurt elevated her beyond both Mr. and Mrs. Weese in height, her long legs wouldn't fit in the space between the commode and the door. The porcelain tub was tiny. She could barely cross her legs and fit in it. When Mr. Weese installed a utility sink in the barn, she started washing out there. Soon thereafter, she left the mudroom porch at the back of the house with the flimsy wooden cot and moved out to the barn, which was larger than the house. With scraps of wood, she made herself a wider, longer bed frame. She stuffed straw into a mattress and nailed a folded blanket over it. In the barn, she could stretch and have all the privacy she wanted. She oversaw the animals anyway; their warmth and their sounds were her comfort while the Weeses tended to themselves inside. When she was older and required no watching over, they came to ignore her for most of the day, as long as she went to the reservation school during the morning and did her daily chores in the afternoon. She ate supper with them in the evening and helped clean up the dishes, saying little. When she did speak, it was in German. She'd do her daily business in the toilet, then head out to the barn to sleep. She had enough free time to practice her reading and think about numbers, rearranging them in her head. Until she acquired notebooks, she counted and drew pictures on the stall walls.

Kay learned how to make ceramic bowls from a Hopi girl named Sue at the reservation school. Someone had donated a kiln, and it stood out back behind the school. Sue shared the secrets of how to create bowls and dishes. When she moved away, Kay felt sadness and her first stab of loneliness. For Sue, Kay practiced making dishes and bowls. She liked painting geometric patterns around the rims. After a year, she thought she was pretty good at it, and she kept her stack of plates and bowls on a shelf in the barn.

The running of the farm functioned around the expectations of the season with a purpose that Kay never questioned. When Mrs. Weese coughed up blood and spent a week in the infirmary, Kay hadn't accompanied Mr. Weese. She stayed back and managed the farm. Eventually, a coughing spasm took the life out of Mrs. Weese. Kay was nineteen, and she surmised she'd had a pretty good life up to this point.

In the truck, the calves next to her shit in the straw and the smell taunted Kay's nose. She thought about Sally's comment on her body odor. At the barn's utility sink, Kay had sponge-bathed daily with bar of gritty soap. At the yard pump, she washed her hair once a week. Since Mrs. Weese's passing a couple of years ago, she hadn't been too dedicated to cleanliness. She realized it had been a week since she last washed her body parts and a month since she had washed her hair. She blushed. Sally was right; she should take better care of her body. She liked soaking in that long bathtub at Aunt Bernice's.

The truck sashayed down the switchbacks of the Black Hills four miles to Clarkdale. In the back, Kay bounced and held onto the calf. She pulled the bandana around her neck over her nose to keep from breathing in the dust that the truck tires kicked up. A feeling of emptiness pervaded Kay. She wondered how, with all that had happened, she could feel nothing. Something was wrong with her. Something was missing.

She thought about how Mr. Weese had changed after his wife's death. He found an enthusiasm for life he hadn't shown before. He talked excitedly on the phone to his landlady, Connie Vandenberg, about her hair-brained idea. It was Prohibition, and she wanted to make a deal. For a cut of the profits, she wanted him to store the bootlegged rum at the farm. Mr. Weese agreed to pick up the deliveries in Phoenix once a month and store the smuggled cases in the barn. Sometimes he arranged for the cases to be forwarded to her hotel in Chicago by small plane, and other times he drove up a case or two to her sister Bernice in Jerome. The plan turned into a mess that got him killed. Kay recalled George Hero firing the gun. When Mr. Weese collapsed, it was like looking at a telephone pole falling down, ending with a slow, loud thud. It bothered Kay that she did not feel sad about that. What was she to do now that she was alone? What about the farm and the animals?

Yesterday, she met Sally and was thunderstruck. Here was someone close to her age and full of emotions who engaged in conversations with her. Sally was the warm and demanding sun, while Kay was the tree lizard, bland and blinking. Sally was the monsoon rain promising life with her explosive energy. She sealed the cracked earth and forced the desert flowers to open and blossom. Sally did not look at her like she was tall and ugly. Kay's feelings for the Weeses were pushed back to make way for the need to stand in the sun and drink the rain.

Also, Kay followed Sally around because of the gold-plated pistol. She had decided on the way up to Jerome last night to keep the luger for herself. Fanciful inlaying wrapped around the gold-plated cylinder like dark vines. The gun was nothing like the lusterless shotgun at the Weese farm. She imagined an accomplished gunsmith had created the pistol just for Jonathan Vandenberg. She had intended to put it in the bag that contained the possessions he wanted to give Sally. Instead, Kay had placed it in her own bag, the one with the red Road Runner woven on the flap. Just for a bit. It was a chance to admire something beautiful for a while. Besides, what if Sally's bag was stolen? *Setze nicht alles auf eine Karte.* She heard the Weeses echo in her mind, telling her never to keep all her eggs in one basket. She'd protect it well.

The driver descended the dirt road. She felt the shape of the gold-plated pistol from outside the bag. Kay listened to Sally making the driver laugh. Eventually, the driver stopped the truck at the lane of the Weese farm next to the Verde River. Sally told Kay she'd decided to go to the hospital to visit her father. She promised she would stop by later to pick her up. Kay waved goodbye and walked down the lane, which led to the single-story house with a veranda under tall, shimmering trees. Marvin, the horse, greeted her at the fence. She met him and patted his cheek. On her side of the fence, she found some long grass and pulled a clump for him to chew. She would need to feed the animals soon. At the front porch, Kay stopped and listened. There was a loud truck approaching behind her.

Dahteste, an Apache grandmother, drove up in a black truck with her son and grandson. Dahteste called her adult son the Apache name Tarak even though he was Navajo. She'd adopted him after a horse had kicked him in the head as a boy. His eyes had a tendency to roll when you spoke to him. His family had made plans to move a far distance away. They left Tarak at the school where an agreement was arranged between the family, the principal, and Dahteste that she would care for him. He was eight at the time. This Dahteste had explained to Kay freely. Tarak was thirty now, with pointy cheekbones and a long, slender nose. His skin was the color of wet bark. Tarak smiled a lot but didn't speak much. He had a gift for weaving and spent his time at the loom making saddle blankets and handbags with flaps. The loom stayed at the entrance of Kay's barn, where Dahteste could keep an eye on him while she worked. She sold his blankets and her dried apothecary to travelers who passed through the valley. She made a meager living. The grandson was a boy named Elan. Dahteste had adopted him a few years ago by verbal agreement in much the same way as she had with Tarak. This time, a Hopi mother had died during childbirth. Elan was ten and alone. Dahteste said her heart and mind were sharp, but her joints throbbed and grinded painfully. Her hips hurt. She could barely lift her left arm, and the world was blurry. Her boys, she told Kay, were her helpers.

"This is my tribe. We bear the burdens of life together and get by."

To Kay's annoyance, Dahteste talked too much by confiding in Kay when she shouldn't have. By offering Kay her opinion when it wasn't asked for and expecting Kay to respond. By assuming the shared intimacy granted Dahteste license to probe and advise Kay when she never agreed to such a friendship. It was tiring to keep her distance. It was tiring to pretend she cared. After Mrs. Weese's passing, Mr. Weese had hired Dahteste to help Kay around the farm. Kay wasn't sure if he wanted to help them out of pity or because they came cheap. They arrived during last year's harvest season and stayed throughout the winter. They repaired the outbuildings and cleaned the grounds. Kay showed Dahteste how to can the fruit and vegetables and store them in the cellar. They came to the house three days a week and Mr. Weese paid Dahteste three dollars each visit. Now that Mr. Weese was gone, Kay was not sure what to do. Connie Vandenberg owned the property. Who knew what she was going to do with them or the animals or the farm? Dahteste hummed at the far end of the house in her rocking chair. It sat on the dirt and faced the road and the barn. She watched Tarak move the shuttle stick right to left, weaving the yarn through the pattern while the batten stick kept the weaving tight and the rods divided the parts of the design. In a few days, Tarak would have another saddle blanket finished.

Kay did not like Dahteste. She nagged Kay to harvest the desert plants and to teach her Apache secrets. Kay wasn't interested. Dahteste soaked reeds for basket-making and pulled her over to show her how to weave. Kay still wasn't interested. She sat Kay down next to her when she took out her grinding stone and mulched the dry Creosote bush into a powder. She explained how the powder would alleviate the pain in joints. Or she would tell Kay, "You can take the dried stems and boil them down into a poultice, or you can use the leaves for a tea. Make it stronger to combat the breathing sickness and monthly cramps."

Dahteste took out a branch with a green paddle and clusters of grape-like fruit lining the top of the paddle. "This is the jojoba plant. The fruit produces an oil with many purposes. I will show you today how to make shampoo. Use it. Then, I will show you how to prepare it into a salve to help heal skin sores."

"I don't have sores, old woman."

"You must be ready. Just like the Weeses' garden and orchard, where you gather the fruits and vegetables and store them in the cellar, preparing for winter. Why is this concept hard for you? Are you stupid as well as dirty? When you are sick or have an ailment, the desert will take care of you. These secrets are passed down from one mother to another. I am willing to show you. Do not be thick-headed."

"I don't want to know the Apache way. I am Hopi."

"You were born Hopi but don't know the stories. You do not speak Hopi. You are like the gray cloud that has no shape."

"Maybe, old woman. But at least I'm not Apache."

Dahteste spat and went back to work, pounding the soggy stem with a stone that was shaped to the contours of her weathered hands and stained the color of olives.

Kay wanted to tell the old grouch to leave, but she thought Tarak

and Elan worked well, and if they didn't help with the general maintenance of the farm, who would? She admitted she was exhausted trying
to do everything herself. Last week, Kay and Dahteste fought again.

"You say you are Hopi, but you walk around speaking German and
English. You say you are Hopi, but your hair is not coiled over your
ears. You eat out of jars and cans. You are the Weese's dog."

Kay punched Dahteste in the shoulder. "Go away, old woman!
Where is the family that would teach me these things? Why did they
go? I know you and your Apache killed them, and I was left by the side
of the road! The Weeses took me in and cared for me."

"Is that what they told you? The Apache killed your family?"

"Yes. I have the newspaper clipping. It was 1905. The Apache were
angry and wanted to stretch the boundary of their land in the valley.
They demanded the Hopi leave. Many were killed. I was five years old.
My mother and sister died, and I was alone."

Dahteste grabbed a piece of long grass rising up against the white
boards of the house and chewed on the end. She looked at Kay with
black, cold eyes. Her face had ripples of wrinkles from her forehead to
her chin. Her throat dangled with loose skin. Kay wondered how old
she was. Seventy? Eighty?

Dahteste finally responded, ignoring the accusation. "Those Weeses.
Did they love you?"

"They taught me their ways. I was happy with the farm. My animals. This is my home."

Dahteste announced, "It was influenza that took your family. Not
the Apache."

"Shut up and clean up your mess. You know nothing."

Kay pulled out three dollars from a small tied purse attached to her
belt. "Here is your pay. Go away. Both Weeses are dead, now. I don't
know what the owner will do with the farm."

Kay bit her lip and forced the tears back. She walked to the front and up the porch steps, slamming the door as she entered. She looked around the living room. She looked past the wing chair and the couch. By the kitchen door, the dinner table with four chairs shined from a recent polishing. The rooms felt empty. She went to the back bedroom that the Weeses once occupied. Since Mr. Weese's death, Kay had scrubbed the sheets and blankets and aired the pillows. She'd removed their clothes and burned them out back in the burn pile. Yesterday, she decided to move in to the bedroom after she sampled the comfortable mattress and downed pillows. It was time to leave the barn and act like an adult.

Outside, the doors to the truck slammed shut. The engine sputtered and feebly came to life. Kay listened as they left the farm. When all was silent again, she went to the bottom drawer of the walnut dresser and pulled out the kachina doll she had been holding by the side of the road when the Weeses had discovered her and taken her in. It was carved into the shape of some god she didn't know. A face stained blue with a smile. Frayed corn husks for hair. A sash tied around a long waist. Her eyes filled with tears and she whispered meaningless words, Hopi words, lines from an old lullaby, perhaps. She did not know. She could faintly remember sitting on her mother's lap, the shadow of another running around her. Her sister. The woman's voice was muffled and soft in pitch, and she wondered if she did not dream them. She liked to dream about them. They were ghosts from her past who visited her with laughter and songs. She felt them, her mother and sister, more than she pictured their faces. They were a warmth that consoled her. A feeling of love when she awoke in the barn, and the cow mooed in the back field, and Marvin breathed loudly in the stall next to her bed.

She put the kachina doll gently back and shut the drawer. She turned and looked at her neatly made bed, knowing that Mrs. Weese would have approved of the straight angles of the sheets at the corners, the plumped pillows in the bleached pillow cases, and the quilt made of faded pink and green pinwheels lying flat across the bed. She put her face in her palms and cried.

* * *

Kay made herself a kind of holster out of leather straps and fastened the gold-plated pistol to the thin part of her thigh. The extra material from her gauchos hid the shape of the gun. She wore it constantly, liking the feel of the gun against her skin.

It wasn't that day but a week later when Sally arrived at the farm. She brought with her Jonathan Vandenberg. Sally went inside the house to freshen up in the bathroom. It was Mr. Vandenberg's first time out of the hospital, and he asked to take a walk. Kay obliged, and they walked slowly to the orchard. His hand touched his bandaged shoulder while they walked. The Weeses had started the orchard a decade ago, and their devoted labor resulted in four long rows of fruit trees. Crop yields produced persimmons, peaches, figs, and apples. Last year, they had planted a short row of avocado trees that produced a puny amount. It was a start. Kay loved eating the green pears by scooping out the fleshy inside surrounding the large pit. After canning what fruit they would need for the year, their harvest was sold to a local merchant who shipped the produce on the train. Some shipments went around the mountain to Prescott and then down to Phoenix. Other times, the line ran to St. Louis and Chicago.

Kay escorted him to the back fields where the horses and the dairy cow grazed during the day. She introduced him to Marvin, who neighed for attention. She led Mr. Vandenberg back to the front porch, shooing the chickens away with her foot as they clucked and poked for food in the grass. Kay made a mental note to corral them in their coop and lock them up in the hutch; it was the time of year when coyotes started migrating. At dawn a couple days ago, a few had jumped over the wire fence and entered the farmyard. They claimed two chickens. She had heard their shrieks and went running outside with the shotgun, but she was too late. She saw one carry a dead chicken in its mouth as it ran up the lane. Pesky bastards.

Kay's attention shifted to Mr. Vandenberg. The walk had weakened him. He was having trouble climbing up the front steps to the porch. She smiled and offered her elbow for support.

"Here, Mr. Vandenberg. Sit here." The rocking chair proved too difficult for him. He held his shoulder and gasped, clutching the porch railing. "I'll just lean here. Since the surgery, seems I can only stand or lie down."

He closed his eyes and exhaled slowly. The two were quiet.

Kay let her mind wander. She listened to the horses, who meandered into the barn to escape the heat, snorting and whinnying, complaining she was late serving their daily portion of grains. She envisioned the far back pasture next to the river, lined with Sycamore trees, where old Marvin and the milking cow stood in the water to keep cool. It was breezy today. Kay focused on the leaves rustling in the trees. She imagined she heard the river flowing over the rocks and around the bend, where the cattails grew tall and impregnable. She envisioned a plump largemouth bass bumping over the rock bed and felt the cold water push at her calves. Later, after the sinking sun hid behind Mingus Mountain, she would walk to the bank and try to fish. She'd have a good hour before the darkness claimed the day, when the coyotes would yip and dare to catch one of her chickens. For now, it was midday and too hot. She broke from her daydream. She supposed Sally and her father would want lunch.

Kay went inside and poured Mr. Vandenberg a tin mug of cooled tea. She knew he was in pain, so she included the distilled juice from the agave flower stalks. Dahteste had shown her how to make it, and Kay liked the intoxicating effects.

"The Mexicans call it tequila, but the Apache call it *pulque,*" Dahteste told her. It didn't matter to Kay what it was called. After a day's work on the farm, her muscles ached, and she enjoyed sipping some to relax. So far, it was the best discovery of Dahteste's teachings. Afterwards, Kay had begrudgingly grown curious about the medicinal remedies of the desert.

Sally came out of the bathroom and went to the front porch. Kay cut up an apple and spread Beech-nut peanut butter on sliced bread. She used up the last of the strawberry preserves. When she returned to the front porch, Sally sat in the rocking chair, gripping the armrest.

Sally said, "I don't want to go back to her."

Mr. Vandenberg's smile was tight. "Jerome is not a place for a young lady. You know your mother would help you if you insist on a career of dancing and acting."

Sally groaned. She looked at Kay, somewhat embarrassed. "Kay doesn't want to hear this baloney." Sally inhaled from her diaphragm and held it.

Kay held the tray of food and waited. She squinted at the lilac bush at the side of the front porch. The blossoms were long gone, but the abundant leaves waved in the wind. The heat from the sun had wilted them. Kay muttered to the bush, *"Ich muss dich wässern."*

Sally boiled. "How can you stand to be with her? You would have been a great artist by now if she hadn't sent you away." She snapped her head to Kay. "And you, what's with all the kraut-talk? I thought you were an Indian."

"Stop it, Sally. You're being rude." Jonathan looked exasperated. He accepted a sandwich and took a bite and chewed. He surveyed the property and looked solemnly at Kay.

"I'm sorry about Mr. Weese. Do you have plans, now that you are by yourself?"

Kay didn't know what to say.

Sally asked her father, "What's Connie going to do with the property?"

Kay held her breath. He replied, "I don't know what your mother is going to do. She's on her way, you know. You'd better be civil."

Sally scoffed. "What does she want with this farm, anyway? What's she up to?"

His face clouded over. "Ask George. I know nothing."

"This is my home," Kay blurted out. She pressed her knees together and felt the hidden pistol between her legs. They both looked at her and smiled sympathetically. Kay went inside and sat down on the couch. She could see them through the screen door and hear their conversation.

Jonathan Vandenberg strained to breathe. "Sally, I'm going back to New York City. Please come with me." He held his shoulder and arched his neck in pain.

Sally answered, "I don't know what Mother has George doing, but it's not a good sign that he's here. I saw the crates of liquor in the barn. Is she supplying Aunt Bernice with rum? Is that why she wants the farm, as a cover?

A hard tone entered his voice. "Like I said, Sally. I've always been in the dark."

"I suspect George has been ordered to take me back to Chicago."

His voice was thick with emotion. "Wouldn't you rather go back with me?"

Sally wouldn't take the bait. "I'll take my chances. I don't care what George says or does. The only place I'm going after here is Hollywood. You go, Dad. I'll be okay."

He wouldn't look at her. "Still no sign of George's pistol?"

"No, I truthfully have not seen that pistol of his anywhere."

Kay tensed up. It was an ambiguous answer as she watched from the couch. Sally ran her hands over her bare arms and straightened the creases of her flowered dress. Her hat had a feather in it, which bounced in the hot breeze.

"You think George came to get me or the pistol?" Her voice changed, sounding afraid. "I think he'd kill anyone who had it. Mother told me it once belonged to Fritz Lang, the German movie director. How did you have it, Dad?"

"Your mom arranged for me to paint a portrait of William Clark's grandson, Billy. I thought it would be a good prop for the commission, so I took it from your mother's collection room. I didn't know it was

George's or that he'd shoot me over it. Poor Mr. Weese. He took the bullet and my shoulder is shattered."

"Dad, she arranged the commission so you could check up on me."

"That, too, yes. You are our daughter."

Sally looked away and changed the subject. "George staged it so that it looked like Mr. Weese shot himself after he shot you. Why don't you tell the police the truth?"

Mr. Vandenberg coughed and limped toward the Model T. "Take me back to the hotel, please." He was sweating and looked pale. He slowly inhaled and announced, "Your mother is arriving the day after tomorrow."

Sally said, "Wait, Dad. What about Casper? How is he doing?"

Jonathan turned and faced Sally. "He's okay. Still working as a doorman."

Sally shrugged her eyes. "No, I mean, is he happy?"

"Who is?" Jonathan took out his handkerchief and wiped his brow. "I know he misses you. He always asks about you." A pause. "He lost his family a long time ago. I think he thought of you like kin."

Sally looked thoughtful. "I feel foolish I never asked him about his family. All I know is that you two have been friends since you were a boy."

Jonathan smiled. "Yes, well, that was a long time ago, too. When I was old enough and moved to Chicago, I searched and found Casper and his family. His wife Clementine came down with the influenza around 1915, I think, and his son Pete went off to the war and was killed there."

"That's sad. What will become of Casper, I wonder? His leg is pretty deformed now, isn't it? What will happen when he can't do his job? Will Connie fire him?"

Jonathan sighed, tiredly. "You keep asking questions for which I have no answer."

Sally stood and carried the tray inside to the kitchen. Kay followed her. Sally leaned her palm on the porcelain sink and wiped tears from her cheeks with the other. She took a deep breath and exhaled and stood thinking for a bit. Kay watched her quietly while she got her composure back.

With a conspirator's whisper, Sally said, "If it's really what you want, I can help you stay on this farm so you can keep the orchard and the farm running."

Kay blinked several times. "I have to settle affairs at the bank to-morrow morning and figure out what kind of situation I'm in. I have work to do, Sally. The animals need tending. I need to flood the orchard and this house needs cleaning."

"How long are you going to live here all by yourself? You're nuts. And by the way, what in the hell did you do with George's pistol?"

Kay turned and looked through the hallway out the door. She watched Mr. Vandenberg climb gingerly in the passenger side of the Model T. *Was für ein hübscher Mann.*

She refused to answer Sally, and a long silence followed.

"Oh, hell's bells. Keep it, for all I care. I'll talk to my mom and con-vince her you can stay and run the farm. If you want to hold onto this place, I can help you."

Kay was weary of the conversation. She grabbed the can of earth-worms at the back of the refrigerator and went out the front door to the car and shook Mr. Vandenberg's hand. "It's been nice seeing you." She walked away and headed toward the barn. Sally stood on the porch and leaned over the railing and shouted at her.

"Tomorrow then, I'll come get you at nine. We'll go to the bank together. Where you going?"

Kay's tall frame was swallowed by the shadowy mouth of the barn. "I'm going fishing."

When she heard them drive away, she exited the barn into the sun with her pole. As she walked down a worn path to the river, a wild burro, hidden in the bushes at the edge of the property, stared at Kay.

Burros from the mine got away or were let loose. Some of them were confused after life as a beast of burden. They wandered the streets of Clarkdale and aimed for the grassy park that Mr. Clark had put in his company town. Sometimes Kay would walk by and see three or four of them nibbling the sod before someone chased them off. The town officials erected a wrought iron fence around the perimeter to keep them out. Last year, one burro strayed over to the Weese farm and loitered near the other animals. Kay didn't mind. Marvin tolerated it, and she suspected he liked the company. Marvin followed the burro as it came out of hiding to walk behind Kay, who led the comical parade. Kay crossed the pasture and headed past the irrigation ditch that allowed her to flood the orchard and the yard during drought season. Suddenly, Kay heard the burro's screech as he stomped and kicked at something in the wild grass. Marvin whinnied and leaped away from the burro faster than she'd seen him move in months.

Kay stepped off the path and dodged the large rocks and the agave plants. She heard the rattle of the snake while the burro stomped on it. Kay patted the knife attached to her belt and dropped her fishing gear. The snake slithered away, weak. Kay picked up a rock and smashed its head. Then she pulled out the knife and severed it. She put the body around her neck like a thick rope. It was cool and the scale tips were sharp. She rattled the tail tip rhythmically and resumed her trek to the river. If she didn't catch any fish, she'd fry up the rattlesnake for supper instead. The burro ran away and disappeared into the bushes.

At the bank, Kay sat on a rock under partial shade and dipped her fishing line into the swirling, brown water. The sun's heat radiated on her exposed shoulder. She pressed her knees together. Inside the leather band was the gold-plated pistol. Her skin was moist with sweat and it molded the holster to her thigh. The pistol emanated a sensation within her, a mixture of guilt and excitement, for the secret treasure was not hers to keep, but she couldn't bring herself to give back something so exquisite. She told herself she was borrowing it for a while and would return it. Soon. She reached up into the wide leg of the gaucho and pulled out the pistol. Her fishing pole propped up against a tree waiting to bend to a catfish or bass.

The carvings etched into the grip of the Colt luger pistol compelled Kay to run the tip of her finger over the intricate leaves and tiny acorns. Smooth wood the color of butterscotch framed the design. Shiny, gilded leaves bordered by an interlocking series of triangles girdled the barrel and trigger. The gold-plated pistol reflected the sunshine and she squinted. Kay peeked into the muzzle and turned it upside down. She wondered if it held bullets and wiggled the muzzle lever open. It was jammed. Gently, she rocked the lever like a tooth resisting an extraction. It released. She opened her palm with her other hand, expecting to catch bullets.

Instead, sixty cut emeralds, polished and crystalline, filled her palm. What stood out amongst the translucent jewels was one dark pink stone. Kay had grown up hearing miners talk about the elusive red beryl found in the Utah mines, but she thought they were joking. She never thought she would be holding a red emerald.

* * *

The next day at the Clarkdale Bank, Mr. Isaac Floch rolled up to them in a wooden wheelchair inside the bank lobby and shook hands with Sally. He then reached over and shook Kay's hand. His grip was moist and warm. Kay politely put her hands behind her back and wiped them on the back of her gauchos.

"Come on, ladies, let's go back here." They passed the teller's ornate window, past a room that contained a large safe and entered his office in the back. He shuffled through papers. He was thin and small in his wheelchair, but his voice was strong. "Looks like the property was leased to the Weeses by Connie Vandenberg. Their agreement, according to the lease, was sixty percent of their profits from orchard-ing. They had a twenty-year lease with a stipulation of a five-year grace period to plant the trees and reap a harvest. The Clark railroad would buy and ship their produce based upon a five-percent markup. In four of the last six years, they made a profit. The drought last spring halted production. Mrs. Vandenberg's attorney has a note here saying the lease will expire in two years. If there is no sizable profit this year, they have the right to evict you and pursue other options for the property. I'm sorry, Kay.

The right to evict me. What a waste, Kay thought, mumbling, "*Alle die ganze Arbeit für nichts.*"

Mr. Floch blinked at her. Sally leaned back in her chair and crossed her ankles. Her cream-colored dress made her waist tiny. Her exposed neck and upper chest glistened from the heat of the morning.

Sally asked, "How much would it cost to buy the parcel of land? My mother *is* Connie Vandenberg. She has done business with William Clark III. She bought the property from him."

"Are you saying you'd like to buy the place? All twenty acres, in-cluding the orchard?"

"I'd like you to look into a purchase price and let me know."

"This is unorthodox. Shouldn't I be talking to Mrs. Vandenberg or her business manager?"

Mr. Floch looked at Kay and held his gaze. Kay noticed a warmth in his eyes behind circular spectacles. She looked down in her lap. What was she doing here, thinking that Sally would buy the ranch? And then what? Rent it to her? Would she sell it to her? How would she pay for it? Kay wanted to hold the title in her hand. First things first. How much?

Sally stared at her. Kay felt her face flush and asked before she lost her nerve, "Why can't I finish what the Weeses started? I planted half those trees myself. I'm the one that helped install the irrigation system. Helped hire migrants and harvest the fruit and picked the walnuts my whole life."

Kay stood up. Her hands were shaking. The gaucho material clung to her backside. Indignation and pride bubbled up from her stomach to the back of her throat, and from her mouth came the outpouring.

"I've birthed, raised, and slaughtered the animals. I've kept the books. Ordered the feed and seeds. Called the train company to pick up the fruit. I've canned the fruit, baked the bread, hoed the garden, and shoveled the shit." She took a breath and held her hands behind her back. In a calmer voice she announced plaintively, "I deserve the farm. I wasn't their blood daughter, but I worked harder than any daughter could have. If the farm fails, it'll be because I've failed. Not because Mrs. Vandenberg kicked me out." She looked squarely at the banker behind the table.

The warm air rattled the opened window pane. Mr. Floch tapped his pen into the palm of his hand. His voice cracked from the lack of moisture in the air. He replied to Kay, "How about if I come out in a few days and visit the place, and then let you know?"

Sally puffed. "And me? I'm the one buying it. Shouldn't you be letting me know?"

"Is it your intention that your mother transfer the property to you?"

"It is. And she'll do it. She'll put the title in my name. I'll rent the farm to Kay. And if the orchard works out, I'll take my cut of the profits."

Kay stiffened. *If* the orchard works out. And if it doesn't?

Sally leaned toward Kay. "You'd be better off having me for a land-lord than my mother. You and I are friends."

Kay sighed heavily. She realized they had something in common. *We both don't want to be beholden to someone else.*

* * *

The sun rose and emblazoned the dawn sky with splashes of crimson and gold. The Weese's truck barely worked, and Kay was leery of driving it. Mr. Weese had liked to tinker with it, but he never seemed to fix it. As Kay slowly made her way the few miles to downtown Clarkdale, she decided to leave it with the mechanic at the Clarkdale Gas Station and pay the bill with money from the Weese checking account. Mr. Floch at the bank worked with a lawyer and released their assets to her for the exclusive running of the farm. She was surprised to learn they had saved 4,000 dollars. Across from the mechanic was the mercantile store. Kay would pick up dry goods and then wait in the park for the truck to be fixed. She was out of bread and wanted to get back to the farm so she could get some dough rising. Sally had asked her if she'd cook while her parents and whoever else showed up at the farm. Kay knew that meant George Hero. She accepted money from Sally to buy groceries. She wasn't looking forward to serving the owners of her own home, but cooking them supper would keep her distracted. She didn't want to make small talk.

Kay stood outside the store with a flour sack and a paper bag of kitchen goods. A few doors down, Mr. Floch rolled out of the bank. With him were three men. Two were in black suits with cowboy hats, and the third looked like a rancher in jeans, a plaid shirt, and boots. When they passed by Kay, Mr. Floch smiled broadly at her and stopped the men.

"Hey, Mr. Howard, weren't you looking for more Indians for your picture? This here is Kay. She's available."

They formed a half circle in front of her and examined her. Kay instinctively stepped back. Her back hit the glass storefront.

"Kay, hello, I'm Mr. Willoughby. I work for Mr. Howard. He's the director of a film we are shooting out in Sycamore Canyon. *The Thundering Herd.*" He bowed slightly to the man wearing blue jeans.

"That there is Jack Holt. He's the star of the picture. Have you seen any of his other Westerns?"

Kay shook her head no.

"Well, Mr. Floch is telling the truth. We need extras. Are you available to help? Won't take long, maybe a couple weeks is all. You'd be paid, of course."

Kay said nothing.

Mr. Willoughby sighed, pulled out a pamphlet from the inside of his jacket, and gave it to her. "We're shooting tomorrow. The directions are in there. Come if you are interested."

They walked off, pushing Mr. Floch in his wheelchair. He turned and nodded goodbye.

Kay stared at the brochure card with "Zane Grey's *The Thundering Herd*" printed in gold, listing Jack Holtz as the star and William Howard directing. On the back, directions were written to the location site and the start date, June 01, 1928. That was a week ago, Kay thought. She thought of pitching the invitation. Instead, she put it in her paper bag between the bag of sugar and cans of peaches. As she crossed the street to the mechanic with the flour sack on one shoulder and the bag in the other hand, she clicked the inside of her cheek and thought of Sally. Kay muttered aloud, "Sally, you're at the wrong place at the wrong time."

* * *

Kay watched Sally drive down the lane when she returned the next evening. She announced she would stay with Kay until her mother arrived at the farm tomorrow. Kay was surprised how glad she was to see Sally. Kay didn't mind being alone on the farm during the day, but as the dusk brought the long shadows, her sadness grew and consumed her.

It was cooling down outside, but the house was stuffy. Sally carried a carpetbag with a change of clothes and her beauty supplies. She set her bag in the bedroom and told Kay, "We'll share the bed, right?" and came out to the living area wearing a camisole and slip. Sally asked her if she had any liquor and Kay told her no. She was out of *pulque.* She poured Sally a cup of water from the kitchen tap and watched the knob in her throat move up and down as she swallowed. Kay felt a wave of affection flush through her. She hadn't felt grateful to Sally at the bank, just anger that her life was turned upside down. It was nice of Sally to help her, she realized. She didn't have to involve herself in Kay's affairs. And she liked that Sally thought of her as a friend. Kay wanted to please her. She retrieved the movie brochure from the top of her dresser and handed it to Sally. Kay told her they invited her to be an extra on the set. Sally misunderstood, thinking they meant her, and squealed with delight.

"Kay, you must come along with me tomorrow, please! I've got the coupe."

"My truck is fixed. It would handle the dirt road out to the canyon better."

Sally jabbered what she knew about the actor Jack Holt and the director William Howard and what outfit she should wear. Kay had washed her gauchos and shirt and underwear earlier and hung them out on the clothesline. They'd be dry by morning. They went out to the front porch. Sally sat in the rocking chair while Kay perched on the porch railing. They listened to the crickets chirp in the darkness. Sally looked at Kay with curious eyes. "How old are you, Kay? What are you? Yavapai? Apache?"

"I'll be twenty when the winter comes. I'm Hopi." She paused. "You really think you'll make it to Hollywood?"

"I'm going to give it my best shot. After all, why not me?" Another pause. "You know, you're smart. Staying here on this farm isn't your only option. One of my Copper Cuties is moving to Flagstaff to go to that new teaching college. They let Indians in. You could become a bookkeeper or a teacher. My friend Claire said they would let her work off her tuition by milking the cows in the dairy. That had me thinking of you."

* * *

The next morning, Sally rose early and began primping. Away they went in Kay's truck, taking the brochure and heading out to the Sycamore Canyon Wilderness. They drove past the mansion of William Clark III, which sat on a hill overlooking Peck's Lake. They continued past the Tapco Electric company that gave energy to the smelting plant in Clarkdale. They drove for a few miles on the dirt road and came to the encampment where tents, horses, wagons, actors, the director, and his staff moved about, giving and taking directions. The construction crew had built a rudimentary town with the facades of a bank, a saloon, and a hotel.

It was hot. Kay got out of the truck and watched Sally swing her hips and arms as she wandered around the set. They stepped up on the porch and stood under its roof in the shade with twenty others. Sally snapped open her Chinese fan and attempted to evaporate the sweat off her face with small strokes of her hand.

"Which one is he?" she asked Kay behind her fan. "Mr. Willoughby?"

Kay blocked the heat of the sun with her cowboy hat. She stood slightly separated from the others and noticed the director from the bank. He stood next to his cinematographer, who peered into the lens of his black movie camera.

William Howard shouted, "Action."

Jack Holtz, the male lead, sat up straight on his horse. He galloped down the lane toward them and trotted up to the makeshift saloon. Howard coaxed their movements with a megaphone.

The actress came out of the saloon and stepped on the wooden porch. The director said, "Come down now, Lois. Move toward Jack like you haven't seen him in years. You're wondering whether he still cares for you or not. But you don't want to seem overly anxious."

Kay watched the athletic, dark-haired actor dismount his horse and take off his hat. Sally whispered to Kay. "That's him. That's Jack Holt. Isn't he dreamy?"

The man behind the camera turned the crank to roll the film. The actors moved closer to the camera. "Play hard to get...Yes...Nice."

Sally squirmed with pleasure. Kay stood next to her, half-shielded from the sun. She looked around her as everyone silently observed the scene. Mr. Willoughby surprised her by touching her elbow when William Howard shouted, "Cut."

"Ah, you made it, Kay! Great. We'll sign you up now and pay you two dollars a day as an extra. Go meet the other Natives over at that tent. Your scene will be up a little later."

Sally turned to him and smiled sweetly. "Mr. Willoughby, didn't you request me? Don't you need an extra showgirl in this picture? I'm a dancer and could be in the saloon. Those girls in there are just plain Janes. How about me as an extra?"

Kay wondered how she knew that, having just arrived on the set. She'd never stepped inside the saloon, which was nothing more than hammered boards with a doorway and a swinging gait. Who knew who waited on the other side? Kay shook her head. The gall. She presumed that Sally felt every female was a plain Jane by comparison. She wondered, as the ugly Indian, if Sally liked her because she wasn't competition? *That's just mean on my part.* Did Sally have to be the prettiest girl in the room? In this case, the prettiest girl out in the wilderness, surrounded by fake buildings and people pretending to be someone else? *What did it matter?* Sally didn't have to help her. She had been nothing but nice to her. Kay squinted up into the blue sky behind her where a buzzard hawk glided on a thermal over the set.

Mr. Willoughby turned and greeted the director, who was getting ready for the next shot planned at the other end of the placard town.

"Mr. Howard, this here's Sally Vandenberg, sir. She's looking to be an extra in the saloon. You want her?"

Sally blinked rapidly. "I can dance, too, Mr. Howard. You won't regret having me in your picture, sir. Whattaya say?" Sally tilted her head. She dared to tap his forearm.

Mr. Howard sized her up and then touched her dyed black hair. "You got the looks of Clara Bow, and her sassiness, too." He smiled. "Sure, Mr. Willoughby. Sign her up for the three scenes. We'll stick her in the saloon, and she can be an extra during the town shots. Today and for the rest of this week. That oughta do it."

Mr. Willoughby looked at the both of them. "Come on, then, you two. Time's a wastin', and time is money."

After they had signed letters of intent for two dollars a day, Mr. Willoughby sent them to a tent where props and costumes were stored. When they emerged, Sally wore a dress that revealed her shoulders and small waist, while Kay was given warrior feathers and buckskins. She was miserable. A lady brushed her hair until it shined on the back of her shoulders and painted white streaks on her cheekbones. Mr. Willoughby entered the tent to inform them they were to report for the next scene in a half an hour. Kay stood tall and protested her costume.

He tried to explain. "We don't need a squaw. We need more Apache braves in the film."

"But I'm not anything close to being an Apache brave. You never said I was going to play a male Indian."

"You'd rather be the whore in the saloon?"

Sally turned to face him. "Hey, I'm not a whore. I play a dancer."

Mr. Willoughby rolled his eyes and shook his head. "Be on the set in fifteen or leave. You both are extras. Take it and the money or leave without the money." He walked away.

Sally said, "What a creep."

A young man sauntered over to Sally and introduced himself. "Hi, the name's Gary. Gary Cooper." He tipped the rim of his hat and talked like a cowboy in character, "Say, you're a cute filly, if I ever saw one. There's a big shindig in Clarkdale next Friday. The town is saying goodbye to the cast and crew. Make sure you go so we can dance, eh?"

Kay watched Sally's cheeks turn pink with pleasure.

An assistant motioned Kay to stand off to the side with four other males with feathers hanging down their backs like warriors from a tribe Kay guessed did not exist. They wore beads and bangles and carried spears. Three of them were Mexican miners and one was Joe, the Italian who ran the mercantile store in Clarkdale. They joked and lit cigarettes and waited for their scene to ambush the wagon traveling down the dirt lane. Kay stood a few steps away, dejected. Sally moved to the end of the porch after Gary was called to appear in the next scene. Kay noticed another man maneuver himself behind Sally.

Kay had seen that profile before. It was the man who had visited Mr. Weese and shot Mr. Vandenberg. It was the same man Sally saw up in Jerome, the one she tried to hide from. It was her mother's bodyguard, George Hero. The owner of the pistol. She unconsciously squeezed her thighs and relaxed as she remembered she'd hidden the gold-plated pistol back in the barn. Kay crept around the periphery of the cast and crew until she was behind him, close enough to hear his conversation.

"George, get the hell out of here."

"You come with me now, Sally, or I'll ruin your little show."

Sally growled and stepped back behind the partition. Kay positioned herself next to Sally and put her fists on her hips. George looked at Kay with a quizzical expression.

"Beat it. This is personal."

Sally linked her arm with Kay. "She's with me, George. What do you want?"

"Where's the pistol?"

Sally sighed with relief. "I thought you wanted to take me back to Mother."

George was broad-shouldered and musky-smelling. Kay was surprised that when she inhaled his scent, it aroused her. He was in jeans and wore a thin chambray shirt that clung to his chest and arms.

"I don't care where you go." He was fuming. "I want my pistol back. It's an antique. You give me the pistol, and I'll tell Connie you ran away to Hollywood. I'll even give you money to get there. Alright?"

His eyes darted around to gauge his surroundings. He tried to act casual. His lips were full and closed, and his face was without expression. It was his eyes that betrayed the heat of emotions inside of him. Kay sensed the feral power of the mountain lion. A scary gorgeousness. Kay's eyes were drawn to the small mole under his left eye. His hand was on his hip as he looked down at Sally, but he did not make eye contact. Kay thought it odd. Instead, he would focus on a part of Sally, like her shoulder, then tilt his head and study her small breasts, her tiny waist. He moved his left hand, and his fingers played with the belt loop at his hip. Kay observed that his shirt covered the hump on his other wrist. He wasn't wearing a hat, and his sandy hair whipped about in the hot wind. Then he turned suddenly and caught Kay in a stare. Sally prattled on about her parents. George and Kay stood staring at each other while the wind blew, and Sally's voice wrapped the three of them in a cocoon. Kay heard a horse bay. She wished she were at the river, fishing in the quiet under the cottonwood trees. She forced her eyes to drop and kicked at the dirt under her worn black boots. She concentrated on the mesquite bush next to her, then the beavertail cactus with its prickly paddles, then away at the finger ridges of the Sycamore Canyon hills that switched colors from green to red to purple as the sun rose and crossed the Verde Valley. Kay looked up at the azure sky. The turkey buzzard had drifted elsewhere.

There was a clanging noise as crew leaders hit metal tubs like a drum and shouted for people to get in their places. Kay could tell that Sally was considering George's proposition.

"I'll be up in Jerome tomorrow night. I'm a nickel-hopper at the Grand Hotel. Or I might be at the Liberty Theater. They have a creepy film showing. That Fritz Lang film you bragged you were in. *Dr. Mabuse: The Gambler.*"

Sally nudged her in the ribs. "Come on, Kay. I'm not blowing this nifty opportunity. Let's go get into position."

George smirked and rolled his shoulders back and stood a little taller. He wiped his forehead. "I'll find you."

* * *

The days rolled on. Kay filmed her scenes and Sally flirted with Gary Cooper. Kay was used frequently as an Indian extra, changing clothes and hairstyles each time, much to her annoyance. The only good thing about the whole experience of *The Thundering Herd* was the money she earned. When she was bored, waiting to be shuffled here or there, she studied how Sally and Gary's flirtations grew bolder. She didn't know where else to stand, and their dalliance was more entertaining than making idle conversation with the cast and crew. By the third day of filming, he began touching Sally. A squeeze here and there. A massage to her shoulders at the end of a day of filming. He played with her earlobe and chatted about his life growing up on some farm in Montana. Kay stood a few steps away, feeling like a wooden carving of an Indian chief at a souvenir store. She was an interloper to their conversations. After a kiss, Kay heard Sally tell him if Howard didn't pick her up for the next movie, she was running away to Hollywood.

"You better take your friend. There's not a lot of Indians to hire and the studios enjoy making Westerns. She's not that bad really. The two of you might make it."

"I'd rather have her for company than George."

"George? The stiff one with one hand? Do I have competition, Sal?" He squeezed her hand.

Sally puffed air out of her pouty lips with disgust. "Good grief, no. He belongs to another. What about you? What are your plans?"

He swept his fingers through his dark hair. "Zane Grey is coming to the party on Friday, Mr. Howard said. I like doing Westerns and they have made quite a few together. Mr. Howard pulled me aside and told me there might be a spot for me in his next picture." He blushed. "He said I look great on film. My face is a charmer."

"You know it," Sally answered and kissed the dimple on his cheek.

Later that evening, after Kay bathed and cooled herself off from the hot day of filming, she went with Sally up to Jerome. Sally chose to dance and earn some change rather than see a movie that had George Hero in it. At the Grand Hotel, a small band played lively tunes in the main lobby. The Copper Cuties showed up. Sally looked like she was having a great time dancing the Charleston and the foxtrot with miners who paid a nickel to have a swing with her.

Kay didn't want to dance, but she was pleased to see a side room with a card game in progress. She gravitated toward the parlor. She recalled Mr. Weese had hidden his love for poker from his wife. He taught Kay how to play variations of stud and draw poker when the occasion offered itself, usually when Mrs. Weese left to visit a relative over the mountain in Prescott. Strange as it was, it was the only real connection Kay had with him. When someone called "Five Card Stud," she impulsively sat down at the table and bought chips with the two dollars rolled in her pocket.

Kay caught sight of George as he stood in the archway between the lobby and the parlor. At the card table, Kay was distracted by his presence and aggressively bid with a pair of threes. George turned his head and saw her. The dealer dealt her another three. She backed off the bet with hopes of luring others to increase the pot. The dealer went around the table and the bet was raised. When it was time to call, Kay grinned. She won the pot of seventeen dollars. George nodded to her, impressed.

In the next few hands, she had slop. But in the fourth hand, she was dealt three spades. As she kept her mouth fixed into a line and didn't move in her seat, she put her elbows on the table and peeked over her cards and watched George. He was in the card room now. He made eye contact and wouldn't release her. She almost missed her turn. The dealer gave her a fourth spade. She bet. The pile of dollars grew. Players folded or asked for another card. She asked for one more. George was standing behind her now. She could feel the heat on her back as though he touched her. The hairs on the back of her neck prickled. When the dealer tossed her a heart, she didn't move a muscle. She bet big. Others looked at her and wondered if she was bluffing. Two folded. Then there were three. Kay instinctively put in all her money. The other two angrily threw down their cards and swore at her. One man called.

And then she lost.

She stood up and said goodnight. They ignored her. Someone sat down in her spot. She felt George's hand on the middle of her back as he guided her toward the elevator. Kay felt dizzy. She didn't say a word. She didn't turn to look at him. When the elevator door closed and the machine carried them up, he twirled her hair and pulled to reveal her neck. He moved his lips to her skin. She felt a thrill when he positioned his teeth over her tendon and playfully bit her. In his room, she was paralyzed. She was almost as tall as George. Her eyes followed his movements as he undressed her. Kissed her. And she stood there, letting him do what he wanted, frozen. It took many minutes before she thawed and responded to him. When she did, their passion was equal.

CHAPTER FOUR

GEORGE

George's instructions were to check the inventory and oversee Weese's movement of the rum cases in the barn to Bernice in Jerome. That was the deal Connie and Bernice had agreed upon for housing and feeding Sally. Four quarterly installments of smuggled rum from St. Maarten, where Connie had finagled a deal with a plantation owner she had taken a liking to during her migratory two-month winter stay. Not enough rum to draw attention to herself, but enough to make a tidy profit and to satiate her elite friends at the Pearson Hotel.

The definitive blow came last year, when Sally confronted Connie and claimed that Bernice was her real mother. That somehow, Connie had leverage and paid Bernice to stay away from Chicago. Connie was barren, and she took Sally away from Bernice and raised her, insisting that Jonathan and she were her parents. So theorized Sally.

George thought it was bullshit. Some of it, anyway.

What he did know was that Connie was so angry with the accusation, she consented for Sally to live in Jerome—temporarily. She would give Sally a year to grow tired of her crass Aunt Bernice, the boarding house, and the trampy lifestyle of the town. The year was now up, and this was the last shipment Connie would deliver to Bernice. After he checked on Weese and the farm, George was ordered to bring Sally back to Chicago, by force if necessary. Connie had given him sedatives to administer to her if she wouldn't submit. George might give them to Sally just to keep her trap shut during the two-day train trip back to Chicago.

Meanwhile, the situation with Weese had worsened. He'd had a change of heart and refused to house the rum. He said the cops were suspicious, and he didn't want the kickback money. George called Connie, and she told him to sever ties and give an eviction notice to Mr. Weese. She sent a surprise reinforcement. Jonathan would join George in Arizona. George figured he returned to Connie from New York only to have her redirect his attention. He imagined she told him to sweet-talk Sally and placate Mr. Weese. It was a mistake. When George arrived a week ago, the situation got complicated. A sudden meeting was called, and George was not in any shape to negotiate with Jonathan or Weese. The three men faced each other at the farm. Mr. Weese threatened he would rat on the Vandenbergs to the cops. Instead of appeasing Mr. Weese, Jonathan tried to act tough. He shocked George by pulling out the gold-plated pistol and started swinging it around. George was so intoxicated he panicked. Would Jonathan try to shoot it and discover the pistol contained emeralds, not bullets? George snapped.

There was Jonathan on the ground, bleeding from his shoulder, and Mr. Weese dead. He staggered over to Weese. George positioned his gun into Weese's hand to make it look like a suicide. He sneered at Jonathan and demanded he please Connie and go along with the cover-up.

"Get up, you sissy; it's only a shoulder wound. Call the police but leave my name out of it."

George was unsure if he could drive but knew he had to get out of there quickly. He fell into the roadster and turned toward Jerome. Something nagged at him. He was forgetting something important. The hit of opium taken earlier was intense, and he was too anaesthetized to remember. It took all his energy to stay on the road. As he ascended the hairpin curves, the dust left a film on his linen suit and distracted his driving. He inched his way up the lane to the Grand Hotel. He barely made it into his room before he vomited violently and collapsed onto his bed. As his eyelids strained to open, it was then he remembered.

He had forgotten to confiscate the gold-plated pistol.

* * *

After discovering the Grand Hotel and the wholesome charm of Kay a few nights ago, he decided to remain in Jerome and drive the four miles to the farm when necessary. George smacked his lips. Nothing beat that enraptured expression when girls found the passion within themselves. Kay was no exception. Besides, he inhaled the whiff of opium permeating around corners and alleyways of Jerome like incense.

He lay in his room recovering.

He reflected on his strange life and the turbulent emotions that shackled him. Since the war, George had developed ways of controlling his feelings. One way to do that was by playing a mental game of thinking his emotions as colors that he could control with an iron fist.

It had been six years since his return passage from Hamburg to Chicago. At first, he had imagined a prison to keep his emotions in. He was the warden and his feelings banged the iron bars to be released. He rattled the skeleton keys on a ring. Anger transformed into a blob of heat, rolling, a fist stretching the inside of a bronze balloon. His shame was the color violet, a bruise for the loss of Mitzi, and the achy lump squeezed through the cell bars to reach for the keys to open the door. Her hazel eyes haunted him. His heart ached fiercely. Therefore, it was the abalone cloud of apathy that George chose to release most days. There was freedom behind his frozen expression and staying numb.

Time flew. The years passed. He forgot about his missing hand. His mental habit of killing Private Cox was a common motion, like picking up the telephone or signing his name, but it lacked the satisfaction it once had. In his mind, he moved down the dank center of his prison, out of reach from his feelings.

George thought Jerome was an atypical pocket of strangeness. The concept of time eluded him. He kept checking his watch and asking the hotel clerk what day it was. It was Wednesday, two days before the farewell party to the film team in Clarkdale. Connie arrived yesterday. She played the masquerade of loving wife and happy mother. It freed up George's time until he was required to attend the party as a body-guard. He steered the coupe to the front of the post office and parked. He looked out at the Verde Valley a mile below and widened his eyes to capture the space before him. Faintly to the right, he smelled opium. It lured him around the corner, and he stopped in front of the Liberty Theater. *Dr. Mabuse: The Gambler* was playing. George chuckled. *So Fritz's film reached all the way to this Wild West town*. He studied the poster and smiled with incredulity. It occurred to him that he never saw the finished version. Would it be safe to revisit the past? He made a mental note of the seven o'clock showing and stood with his left hand in his pocket, jiggling the change. He crossed the street and entered Mr. Yee's restaurant, The English Kitchen.

It took only a couple of questions, and Mr. Yee pointed to his broth-er, who grunted and led him to the backroom pantry attached to the kitchen. A propped open window reflected light and circulated the air. Behind a wall of shelves holding tin cans and sacks of rice was a bed. George took off his linen jacket and gently hung it on a hook drilled into the brick wall. The last thing he wanted was to awaken and find someone had stolen it. Connie had paid a lot of money for it to fit him perfectly. He stashed his breast pocket wallet inside his cotton boxers for protection. George was eager to go under. The anticipation revved his heart, and he practically leaped onto the metal bed with the thin mattress. He took the straw given to him and chased the smoke of the melted opium, inhaling deeply. The world quickly dulled and he was only semi-conscious. Imagined dreams and bent recollections converged. His mind was a movie screen. There were Fritz Lang and Private Cox sitting on stools at the side of the stage in tuxedos and white gloves. George sat in the first row of the theater and watched red velvet curtains separate. The scene unfolded:

George lifted the left leather glove, embossed with the letters G. H., from the hotel dresser and rubbed the soft hide with his hand. Amid a washing and a change into a herringbone travel suit, he listened to the blood gurgling from the woman's neck. Soon the fluid would drip to the floor and the room would turn messy. He needed to leave. Looking into the mirror, he adjusted his premade bow tie and stared at her reflection. She was a small vamp with red lips and long yellow hair. He had met her on the train this morning in St. Louis. She was returning to a relative in Chicago, and he seized her coquettish smile and glued himself to her side on the train, courting her with drinks and chocolate, whispering exotic descriptions of Chicago and the promise of a fine meal upon arrival.

During dinner at the Grand Michigan Hotel, after the waiter presented her a slice of Schwarzwälder Kirschtorte for dessert, he gave her the silver hairpin as a token of his affection. She giggled with pleasure, poked at a cherry from the top of the chocolate cake, and ate it seductively. Then she twisted her yellow hair into a chignon and speared the pick through her knot. Her eyes softened, and he suggested they should drink more champagne up in his room. He managed to escort her to a quiet corner of the hotel lobby and excite her enough to carry her up the service elevator to his room. He unlocked the door and sat her on the bed. He pulled out the silver hairpin and watched her hair drop around her shoulders. He set the pin on the nightstand. He took off his jacket and hung it on a chair deliberately. She fell back, half-dozed and clothed. He leaned over her. Her hair looked like a blanket on the pillowcase, and when his fingers reclaimed the pin, it caught the lamplight next to the bed and gleamed. He maneuvered her head to exaggerate the neck cord. His full lips sealed over her mouth. At that kairotic moment, he rolled fully on top of her and punctured the hollow in her neck with the hairpin. She did not squirm at first. He could hear the hum of her voice rise up through her ribcage and tickle the roof of his mouth like a fluttering moth stuck under a lampshade. His weight pushed down on her ribcage and stifled her resistance. He watched her pupils widen and blacken, and her face wrinkle up, confused. Her eyes bulged and glassed over like marbles. The dilated pupils became a hole he fell into so that when he experienced the space therein, it filled him with an inexplicable relief, and he called out, expecting to find her.

"Mitzi."

When the vamp lost consciousness, he shuddered and released her.

It was eleven o'clock at night, and the doorman who guarded the massive doors of the Grand Michigan Hotel posed in a wooden chair, pretending not to sleep. George lifted his collar and pulled down his fedora. The night hid the moon while the wind whipped around the corner of Dearborn Street. He almost lost his hat, and he quickened his pace, heading north to Connie's hotel, The Pearson. The polished tips of his shoes clicked on the cement sidewalk. The cadence lulled him, despite the howl of the wind.

He recalled the day that altered his life forever. George was back in the trench. A young replacement, who had arrived hours before, looked at him panic-stricken. The private with chestnut eyes and black lashes fell back against the mud wall and discharged his gun. The bullet hit the embankment and ricocheted into George's right hand. He screamed, and his arm dropped. His hand disappeared into a pool of sludge. He gritted his teeth, and shot the soldier dead as a reply. It was the first time he had killed someone. In the tent that functioned as a hospital, the morphine assuaged the burning pain of his hand, and he slipped into a haze from which he hoped never to awaken. They transferred him to a better facility. Dark shadows filled his mind. The corridors of the hospital glistened. The metal bed was cold. The nurses wore white. One nurse kept his mind distracted from the throbbing pain by reading to him. He couldn't remember what she looked like.

He returned to Chicago, to shocked parents who long thought he was dead. The only word of him had been discharge papers sent from the government and a brief message dated five years ago, revealing he had lost a hand and was on his way home. The chintzy apartment on Pearson Street felt hollow. His mother worked within walking distance at the switchboard of the Pearson Hotel, pulling wires from holes and inserting them into different ones for forty-two hours a week. His father still worked in the bowels of the Pearson Hotel, overseeing a variety of functions, like the Kankakee steam boiler and the new electrical gadgets that made the hotel light up above ground. George had grown up in the basement of the Pearson Hotel, required to spend his free time on Saturdays assisting his father in the semi-darkness. He hated how the mugginess of the basement made his skin moist and smelly.

George slouched in the middle of the front row of his dreamy theater, watching himself onscreen in a close-up. The mole under his eye bobbed and his piercing stare flickered as he thought of his father. He envisioned closing the ancient coal furnace with his father in it. Lock the door. Escape. But to what, the Great War? At least it had gotten him out of Chicago and given him a chance to see something different. Like Berlin.

Berlin. No. George on the screen opened his eyes, and his perspective changed. He walked down Dearborn toward Pearson Street in the cold. A few cars rumbled by. In his coat pocket, he tapped the hairpin, cleaned and dry, and picked up the pace. He needed to get inside the Pearson Hotel, Connie's hotel, before someone found his soaked, yellow-haired darling in bed. He clenched his jaw and leaned into the wind.

Scene change. From Connie's point-of-view:

In room 702, she attached a cigarette to a slim, long holder and paced around her suite. Finally, there was a tap at her door, and she opened it to see him standing in the hallway.

"You're late, George."

"Couldn't be helped."

"I need you to be ready at nine. We're flying to California to Mr. Klein's estate."

George pulled off his left glove with the opposite armpit and tossed it to the couch. He tried to kiss her lips, but she turned her chin and averted the advance. She realized how undressed she was. With her free hand, she tried to hide the belly fat that clung to the beige lace peignoir robe. She clenched when he touched her round hips with a prurient enthusiasm. She took her cigarette and stabbed him on the top of the hand. He jerked back, sighed, and sat down on the couch. This was the way she liked him. Simmering but submissive. Cordial, but with fuming eyes.

She laughed at him and pouted. "George, you kept me waiting, and now I'm not in the mood. Be ready by nine to take me to the airport."

George's voice was deep. "What are you up to and for how long?"

Connie walked to her nightstand and grabbed a wooden box. Inside, she took out a satin pouch and tossed it to George. He opened up the sack and whistled. He poured a pile of emeralds into his palm. One red beryl, a rare and dark pink emerald, was the prize. He stared at Connie, astonished.

She was giddy. "Otto Klein is all mine. He phoned earlier from his Venezuelan estate. He's meeting me halfway in California. He'll release the rest of the emeralds to me as soon as I sign the earnest note for 150,000 dollars. I need you there to make sure he honors the deal." She took a drag from her cigarette and modified her posture until she looked unconcerned. She struck a pose as though for a magazine shoot. She peered at him and whispered half scared, half in jest,

"Will his Venezuelan henchmen try to kill me during the exchange?"

George remained silent, considering the question. Connie turned away and bit down on the cigarette holder. She crossed the room barefoot to the bar cabinet. She plucked out ice chips from the ice bucket with tongs and dropped them into a crystal tumbler. She poured scotch and listened to his silence across the room.

Finally he spoke, disaffected. "You've been waiting for this deal since he came to the hotel telling you his mine struck a hearty vein of emeralds. Congratulations."

As Connie droned about the details of the trip, her eyes focused on the burn on his hand. He never touched it or blew on the inflamed, puckered circle. She had spent the last eight years training him. Taking him in after the war, ignoring the nub on the end of his right wrist. She offered to buy him a prosthetic hand, but he declined. When she saw him in the lobby talking to his mother, Connie had been attracted to his size, to his sandy hair and square jaw, and the mole under his eye. Why, he could be in the pictures. She approached him. He was without work. It was all so easy. Back then, she was at the top of her game. Taut. Natural. Convincing. She took him under her wing and offered him a small delivery job of dubious legality to see what moral character he had. She paid him some money. Then came a steamy kiss or two. He was receptive. He didn't mind that she had the power in the relationship. He was hungry in all ways. He wanted as much money as she would toss his way. He wanted to serve her, to learn from her, to be associated with her. She understood after years in the basement, he longed for a life above the ground. He was a sycophant and accepted it as the price of escaping a life of labor like his father. George was her personal companion, her pet; she owned him, and they both knew it.

After a few years, she grew bored with him. Uninspired. Their relationship altered to a darker level as she found dangerous jobs for him to do with the hope there'd be a natural accident, and she would be finished with him. She gained more lines around the face. Her hair needed coloring to hide the gray. The roll around her middle expanded and her rump dimpled. She grew complacent. It might be boring, but it was comfortable to have a trained man who did exactly what she wanted. She could easily predict his moves and thoughts and his polite way of speaking to her, but as soon as he had the opportunity, his passion would scare her in bed. In the end, that was why she continued the relationship. For the control outside of the bedroom and the uncertainty within. She needed him more than her jewel collection, her scotch, her cigarettes, her money, even her daughter.

George absorbed her perspective on their relationship from his seat in the front row of his imagined theater. At the bar cabinet, her fleshy leg protruded out of the peignoir. He stood and retrieved his leather glove. It was true, he knew. Her motivations. Her habits. Her desires. If Connie knew he did not love her, had never loved her, it would crush her. He tucked that realization like a trump card up his sleeve and smiled. He left room 702 with a gentle shut of the door and walked away blowing the stinging burn on the back of his hand. Bitch.

As the velvet drapes swung together to end the show, Private Cox and Fritz Lang clapped vigorously.

* * *

When George woke up from his opium sleep, it was the next morning. Mr. Yee nudged him, his words unintelligible but his meaning clear. It was time to leave. He sat up and the room spinned. When was the last time he had eaten? He went to the bathroom and splashed water in his face and combed back his hair. His eyes were dull and yellow. He sat down at a table in Yee's restaurant and asked for coffee and a sandwich. Mr. Yee brought him chop suey.

He exhaled and shook the nightmare out of his head, vaguely aware of the parts that were true. He drank water and left The English Kitchen. George retraced his steps, passing the movie poster advertised in front of the Liberty Theatre. *Dr. Mabuse: The Gambler* was showing again on Friday night. Maybe he'd catch it then. How many scenes was he in? He couldn't remember. It might be fun to see himself on the screen. George put on his sunglasses to escape the brightness of the sun.

He climbed into the white roadster and drove down the mountain to the Weese farm, making a mental list of the situation. Kay was trying to claim the farm. "Fat chance," he said aloud. The Clarks owned the land. Connie leased the farm and sublet it to the Weeses. If *she* couldn't convince the Clark family to sell her the twenty acres, Kay wasn't going to.

No one was at the farm. He snooped around inside the house. George found the brochure for *The Thundering Herd* on the bedroom dresser. He left and followed the directions out to the Sycamore Canyon. What a twist of fate to find himself on another film set. George saw Sally instantly. There she was, flirting with the director William Hoffman. Since she had moved out to Arizona, she had cut her hair and dyed it black. The fringes clung to her moist neck. George thought she looked like a Louise Brooks copycat but had to concede that he admired her pluck.

He reflected on the strange Vandenberg family and his place in their lives. Over the years, as Sally grew up taking dance lessons, George occasionally transported her from lessons to the hotel if the chauffeur was unable. Sally had always been a pain in the ass. Connie was a tough woman, but when it came to her daughter, she indulged to a fault. She forgot to teach Sally manners. She forgot to teach her anything. Connie waited for her daughter's arms around her neck and the kisses of gratitude to fall on her cheek. She never got any.

Connie had a fascination with *objets d'art*. George was in charge of overseeing and protecting Connie's collection room. This meant a lot of dusting, which he found to be a strangely comforting chore. It was always locked, and he had the key to the door. A couple years ago, Sally had pestered him to let her see the room. It was one of the few times Connie stood up to her daughter and told her it was off-limits. It was George's favorite place to be. In fact, it was in the collections room where he found the courage to resist the urges of his addiction. He locked himself inside when his pining was acute. It was quiet except for the faint ticking of the ornate French mantle clock previously owned by an English duke in the 1800s. The gaudy gold damask drapes and the dark green carpeting reminded him of a lounge club in Berlin. When he flipped the switch to the chandelier overhead, the glass display cases showcased her precious stones, raw and set, swords and pistols, hairpins and Spanish fans. She dabbled without taking herself seriously, which was fortunate because her tastes varied upon her mood, and her collection was a haphazard gathering of emotional reactions at the time of purchase. It was a fun hobby without plan or focus. Because of that, it was not difficult to steal from her. He found a man in Los Angeles who accepted the odd jewel or trinket without asking questions and paid him a fair price. Mr. Eugene Baxter. When Connie sent him to Los Angeles on business, he would take something from her precious room and cash it in. His personal savings increased gradually, becoming his emergency stash for when the time came. One absolute truth he believed in: one day their relationship would unravel conclusively, and he would need to disappear.

Connie repeated certain phrases with all her guests. They were stock stories she shared when it was necessary to impress others with her charitable nature. But George knew it was all part of the manipulation, the postcard image she projected. If her guests realized she was filled with red swaths of anger and strokes of green jealousy, it would have tarnished her image. One story was how she met Jonathan Vandenberg. She had become his patron eighteen years ago, when he walked into the Pearson Hotel lobby and asked to paint her portrait. She liked his pretty looks, and after she saw his talent, she sensed a purpose for him. Though his name carried no clout, she liked that he was young and eager to please. She told him he would have access to those who could pay a commission and ensure he had regular showings. 1910 was a busy year. A whirlwind romance. A marriage. A daughter. The far wall of the collections room was dedicated to his paintings, including one of William A. Clark, the copper magnate of Clarkdale. Distinguished and proud, the eighty-six-year-old man sat for Vandenberg before his death in 1925. Initially, the portrait hung in the hotel lobby and legitimized Jonathan's reputation as a portraitist, giving the appearance that Connie knew important people. Business owners, bankers, and Mayor William Emmett Dever paid him for his services. His clean-cut features attracted wives who convinced their husbands to hire him. For a few years, Jonathan was popular. But as time passed, Connie bartered his talents for business favors. Once she offered his talent to paint the wife in exchange for a lenient inspection of renovation projects in the hotel, like the purchase and installation of the new Kankakee elevator. She furthered her influence by buying shares of the Grand Hotel in Jerome, where she installed another Kankakee elevator, making the Grand Hotel innovative considering it was located in the far reaches of the West. It was a satisfying way for Connie to aggravate Bernice, too, who thought she had escaped her insufferable sister.

Despite his initial success at portraits, Jonathan's still lifes and landscapes were deemed too traditional and left unappreciated by Chicagoans. Meanwhile, George moved in and made himself comfortable. Connie eventually suggested Jonathan live at her father's New York City hotel. Jonathan would have more freedom to paint what he liked and secure jobs on his own. If he wanted lessons in Paris, she would see to it. The sucker bought it.

George enjoyed sitting in a club chair facing the display cases in the collections room. He would sniff the furniture polish in the muffled silence and admire his gold-plated pistol, propped up and displayed on its own stand, taken after Thea von Harbou's round of Russian Roulette. The pistol that Mitzi wrestled him for and had discharged a bullet into her heart. He diverted that train of thought back to Jonathan.

"He is an idiot." He laughed. "I'm an idiot."

George stole a third of her emeralds worth approximately 50,000 dollars, including the red emerald found in Otto Klein's Venezuelan mine. He inserted them in the butt of the gold-plated pistol. Nagging questions bothered George. When he found the pistol and reclaimed the emeralds, would it allow him to escape from her? How much money would it take? He shook his head, disgusted with himself. He had access to more money than the majority of the people in the United States. Where would he go, and what would he do when he was free? The room dimmed in the shadows of the late afternoon. George realized his good looks were the defining force that shaped his circumstances. He admitted Connie had taught Sally something. To be beautiful meant power.

"What do you want?" His voice sounded flat as he drove down the dirt road closer to Clarkdale.

The answer was simple. He wanted Private Cox dead and Mitzi alive. He recognized the irony and smirked. Both were dead, yet both haunted him and were still very much alive in his thoughts. They were two captives in his mental prison. He was the warden. But no matter how many times he opened their cells, they wouldn't escape. He had read Bram Stoker's *Dracula* before the war, and the Gothic tale intrigued him. Sometimes George felt like Jonathan Harker, the naive attorney, trapped in the castle by the Count and preyed upon. Mitzi became his Mina, Private Cox his Dracula. Over the last couple years, George felt more akin to the handsome Count Dracula, preying on the Lucy's, the flirty vamps, drawn to their necks, desiring to penetrate their skin. If Private Cox and Mitzi were the undead in his mind, they were sucking the life out him. His journey back and forth between the

dreamy opium state of being and the awake world of Connie's expectations seesawed his psyche like a lumber saw dividing him in two.

He bolted upright from his daydream and pulled into the Weese lane.
There was a black truck parked by the barn door opening. He pulled into
the dusty lane of the ranch owned by the Clark family. That pistol had
to be around somewhere. Unrelenting questions plagued George. Why
did Jonathan remove the gold-plated pistol from Connie's collections
room? Why did he bring the luger to Arizona? The way he waved it at
Weese as a prop of intimidation suggested to George that Jonathan was
unaware the emeralds were hidden inside. Kay was the one who found
Jonathan lying under the sycamore trees, shot. He must have given it to
her. George didn't know what he'd do with the emeralds when he found
the gun, but not having the gold-plated pistol was like losing another ap-
pendage, which hurt worse than losing a hand. It was too linked to Mitzi.

The Apache grandmother sat in her usual spot at the side of the house
facing the barn. She husked corn and pitched the leaves into a paper bag.
She pulled off the hairs and then tossed the cleaned cob into a large metal
bowl. A boy carried a bucket of Anaheim peppers he had picked from
the garden and set it next to his grandmother. George saw movement in
the shade at the barn entrance. A young man sat in front of a loom held
by a bough of a tree, its ropes holding an emerging pattern. His bandana
absorbed the sweat of his brow. His fingers picked at the loom, drawing
the stick horizontally through the binding cords of cream colored yarn. A
batten stick secured the woolen threads down on the previous row. A basket next to him held large balls of black and red yarn. His fingers moved
automatically while he tilted his head slightly to acknowledge George.
George exited the roadster, took off his sunglasses, and smiled at them.

"Good afternoon," he said.

The old lady spoke in her native tongue at the grandson. The boy
carried the peppers to the kitchen. He was silent, head down, lips
locked, but his dark eyes peered up at George with curiosity.

The grandmother husked corn with bent fingertips. Her head was up, but her eyes were closed as if she preferred not to look at him.

She mumbled, "Hello, mister."

George wondered why Kay kept the old bird to work on the farm. "Kay around?"

"No. Back later."

"I'll wait inside."

She grunted.

He went inside and walked to the kitchen. George leaned forward and opened the icebox. Inside was a quart glass bottle filled with lemonade. He drank it. There was leftover chicken on a plate. He took a leg and munched on it. He returned to the living room.

A cuckoo clock on the wall sounded three times. George heard the grandmother gather her things and yelp to the boy in the garden and the man in the barn. George moved to the front porch and watched them load the truck. The boy sat in the flatbed, staring at him, and they left the property. George listened to the hot wind rustle the tall cottonwoods by the Verde River. A wild burro crossed the pasture of rocks and junipers, the heat driving it to the shade. An old horse with protruding hips followed it.

George returned inside the house to search for the pistol. The quiet pressed against his ears. He made a floorboard squeak. First, he checked Kay's bedroom, going through her dresser drawers, careful not to disturb her folded nightgown and undergarments in the top drawer. At the back of the drawer was a wooden box. He opened it and pulled out some beads on a string. A feather. A plain headband of faded cloth. A chunk of turquoise. A pink quartz. A fly buzzed loudly on the screened window next to the bed. George tossed the trinkets into the box and returned it to the back corner of the drawer. The fly flew away.

From the bottom drawer, he pulled out a wooden kachina doll. The whittling and stain suggested a warrior who was preparing for battle. It had a square blue head with red lips and corn husks for hair. How unique. *Just like Kay.* George wondered if it was from her youth, and if so, why was it hidden away? George turned it upside down and shook it. Nothing to suggest the emeralds were hidden inside the doll. Her unconventional history with the Weeses combined with her Hopi traditions was as strange and exclusive as the doll he held around its ankles. He liked that quality about her. Private and hidden. It gave Kay an air of elegance for which she was unaware. If she realized what Sally did, that beauty was power, Kay could train herself to be more forthright in manner. She could be as bright as the Arizona sun. George suspected Kay would rather shine her rays on one man than seduce all the men in a room or the world on the movie screen. That was another side to Kay's exclusivity that aroused George. He decided he would initiate another meeting and see if she accepted. He put the kachina doll back in the drawer and covered it up under folded clothes. He stood and turned around, eyeing the bare room. The double bed was smartly made with a white-quilted coverlet. He sat on the edge and fingered the honeycomb pattern.

Then, he spent his time foraging through the other rooms of the house, eventually ascertaining the pistol was not in the house. He thought about Kay's time spent with animals, and the barn was just a good a place as any to hide the gold-plated pistol. *Did she know about the emeralds?* The barn was empty. The cow and horses were in the back pasture. He went first to a closet and unlocked the padlock. He pulled out the final case of St. Maarten rum to deliver to Bernice. Then he stood frozen and listened as if he expected the pistol to whisper its whereabouts. He ambled about, letting his fingertips feel the corners and props of the barn. He inspected the tools lined up in the corner. The rake, the hoe, the hammers, the vice grip on the workbench. He ran his fingers over the saddles and halters. He checked in tin cans, buckets, and crates. He pressed his palm on the square bales of hay that were lined up in stacks of three. He stared at his hand, waiting for a tremor or vibration from the pistol, or for the emeralds to rustle and announce themselves somehow. He studied the four stalls on the opposite side of the barn. The stall closest to the mouth of the barn drew his attention. Etched into the wall were swirls and geometric patterns. The dust from the barn filled in the lines to reveal Kay's doodles. Inside the stall was a makeshift bed and a folded wool blanket. He counted nineteen vertical scratches over her bed. George assumed it was Kay's age. He looked at the numerous patterns etched in the walls of the stall. He observed a shelf with a stack of pottery dishes. Work clothes hung on nails. He felt a pang of sadness for her and anger at the Weeses.

He muttered, "She grew up out here in the barn. What a jackass for treating her so."

He left her stall and inspected the neighboring one. Above the entrance was a sign painted with the word "Marvin." He stepped into Marvin's stall, clear of dung, a bucket of water in the far corner. In the other was a flat-topped chest with horse files, chisels, hammers, and brushes lying in a pile haphazardly. George's hand tingled. *Oh, Kay. You tried to make it look inconspicuous, but your orderliness is your downfall. Nice try.* George lifted the top tray and below it, the gold-plated pistol with its intricate leaves seemed to glow in the metal box. George grinned and held it in his hand. He shook it and his expression became one of dismay when no rattle was heard. He swore. Gently he placed the gun back into the box, as much as it pained him. When he found where Kay hid the emeralds, he'd come back and get the gun. For now, she needed to think her secret was safe from him.

That's when Kay and Sally drove up in the Weese's truck. A Model T followed them and parked next to the roadster. He emerged from the barn and stood at the archway by the loom. He looked at the rows of yarn as if he were enthralled by how a horse blanket was made. Jonathan helped Connie Vandenberg climb ungracefully out of the Model T. Her peroxide hair rippled to her chin, and her expensive dress clung to dense curves. Her red lipstick clung to her pouty lip. She patted the leather seat of the roadster and her lips set in a thin line. George's flesh crawled.

He heard her say to Jonathan, "Make sure we change cars with George. This Model T is a piece of shit."

* * *

It was Friday. At William A. Clark's Spanish colonial clubhouse, George assumed his position against the wall of the back observation deck overlooking the stunning valley. The purpose of the evening was to commemorate the founder of Clarkdale, who built a company town for those who worked at the smelting plant and mined up in Jerome. George studied the lines of the multi-colored ridge that led to Sycamore Canyon. The setting sun took with it the heat of the day and the air began to cool. The guests clustered and chatted about the affairs of the evening. It was the fifteenth anniversary since Clarkdale was established. Clark's son and grandson were hosts for the evening and gave obligatory speeches giving tribute to the copper baron and senator who made his fortune in mining, banking, and the railroad. Junior, a philanthropist, who lived in California and had established the Los Angeles Philharmonic Orchestra, saluted Clarkdale successes, such as the nearly completed Clarkdale High School. The Gazebo in the town park proved be a popular center of attraction for town residents to gather and hear concerts in the park. Clark, Jr. summarized the design of the town for the visiting guests.

"Engineers and executives live in craftsman houses on wide streets, and their children swim in the town pool. Below the upper end of Clarkdale, as it slopes down to the river, is Patio Town. There, separate facilities and craftsman homes were built for the Mexican miners and their families. My father's wish was to create a beautiful place to raise a family. There isn't a finer company town in the country." Those in the room nodded their heads and clapped.

The clubhouse contained a lounge room each for the gentleman and the ladies. The building also offered an auditorium, a kitchen, and the large observation deck. The grandson known as "Billy" continued where his brother left off. He announced he would be taking a leadership position running the United Verde Copper Mine. Since he would be spending more time in the area, he decided to build his family estate overlooking Pecks Lake. He would include a nine-hole golf course abutting the lake with a clubhouse of its own. "All are welcome." The audience cheered.

George listened to Billy talk about his love for flying airplanes. He shook the hand of his business partner and buddy, Marcus Rawlins, who managed the Clemenceau airstrip in neighboring Cottonwood. A newspaper reporter and photographer took notes and snapped pictures with large flashes. Billy changed subjects from planes to movies. He compared the Rialto movie theater in Cottonwood to the Val Verde in Clarkdale. He hinted the Val Verde theater's preeminence was assured because he had a deal in the works with United Artists to provide top movies and regular entertainment to Clarkdale residents. The guests clapped some more.

George listened to him half-heartedly. The tribute was becoming a grandstand, and it soured his stomach. He turned away and looked at the view. Cumulus and cirrus clouds shared the sky, flushed salmon pink by the final touch of the sun. Twilight was the best ten minutes of the day, George thought, when the glow fills your eyes. Then the sun disappears, the clouds darken, and the day transforms into night. *Does Kay see the sky this way?*

He focused his attention to Connie, who was a few steps away. She wore a satin gown, and it was too tight. Her breasts billowed out of the corset top. He remembered the first time she wore it several years ago, back when she could pull it off. As she puffed on her cigarette, the lines spiking away from her lips aged her. He looked back at Billy. His hair was slicked back and his dinner jacket was altered to fit his lean frame perfectly. George struggled to listen to the tone of his voice, which stressed the vowels and stopped every few words before continuing with the sentence.

"What was the vision of my grandfather? Electricity in every home. Flushing toilets. Clean water piped into the home." He took a drink of champagne and continued. "The finest homes have telephones. The telegraph office can connect you with the world. A library. I'm proud to be the grandson of William A. Clark, and today we salute him for his ingenuity and love for the people of Clarkdale. Thank you for coming tonight, especially the crew of the new Western, *The Thundering Herd.* What a treat to have a Paramount picture shot and rolled right here in the Verde Valley. Our area of the world may be far away from the metropolises of the country, but in this beautiful wilderness, the Old West continues amidst the modernity of the day. Tradition. Technology. Beauty. It all thrives right here in Clarkdale. Thank you."

Someone shouted, "Attaway, Billy!"

After the guests applauded for the final time, Billy smiled for the newspaper photo and grabbed a new glass of champagne. The six piece ensemble resumed playing, and guests began to dance. George eavesdropped on conversations, which wasn't hard to do since everyone was tipsy. George smirked. Only the Clarks could throw a party and serve alcohol out in the open. *If you owned the town, there was a slim chance the cops would bust this hooch party.*

George sidestepped the crowd and listened to the conversation of a more famous guest of the party, Zane Grey, as he vivaciously entertained the director, William Howard, and Billy Clark in the "men-only" lounge room. He desired to explore the Sycamore Wilderness on a

103

camping trip. George was not interested and meandered back out to the observation deck, where the cast and staff mingled with mining executives and their wives. Sally stood next to the extra, Gary Cooper, his lips positioned in a side grin that accentuated his dimple. He touched his forehead to the top of her shiny bob. The reporter saw them and couldn't resist. The camera flash bulb exploded capturing their image, and the pair laughed.

"You with the picture? What's your name, fella?" the reporter asked.

"Gary Cooper. Yep, this is my first film." He put his arm around Sally's waist and lifted her. "And this here is Mighty Mouse. You're gonna see a lot of Sally in the pictures!"

"You two sure make a cute couple."

Sally winked. "Yeah, don't we? Vandenberg. You right that down. Sally Vandenberg, okay?"

Repulsed, George floated back to the wall and leaned against it.

Framed between two potted palm trees, Kay looked tense in a simple sleeveless cotton smock that fell to her ankles. She wore white ballet slippers. *Sally must have dressed her,* he thought. The color was a faded peppermint, and it accentuated her strong shoulders. Her hair was brushed and her high cheekbones set off her dark eyes, which were clear and alert. George thought she looked pretty in a healthy, robust way. Jonathan Vandenberg stood next to his wife looking spiffy in dress and numb from alcohol. He crossed his chest and tapped his shoulder as if to check it was still there. He winced. Jonathan looked at George with an expression of bravado that he could not hold long. He dropped his eyes and looked away. *What a sap.*

Billy Clark and Zane Grey entered the observation deck. Grey had a high-pitched voice and waved his arms to describe his words. He engaged Billy with his description of the red rocks and canyons and hoodoos he had seen in Utah. He touched the director's shoulder to invite him in the conversation. Zane proposed to William Howard an idea of a script and was certain that Paramount, with whom he was under contract, would fund the film, even though there were grumblings that Westerns were losing their popularity with the public.

"I want to tell a different kind of story."

Howard twisted the end of his cigar between his thumb and forefinger. He squinted at Zane, amused. Zane said loudly to the guests that he wanted to organize an expedition by cutting through Sycamore Canyon and meeting up at the Mayhew Lodge at West Fork, north of Sedona. He explained why in a magniloquent fashion.

"Sycamore Canyon is a perfect film location. It includes the canyons of Sycamore Creek and its tributaries, which are incised deeply into the south edge of the Colorado Plateau. The walls of these canyons are nearly flat-lying sedimentary Paleozoic and Mesozoic rocks. They form cliffs, steep slopes, and benches. The hues of day, gentlemen, change constantly, making it a cinematic treat. It's a superb place for ambushes and action sequences. For the drama that unfolds from the plot of my stories."

Waiters walked by with trays of hors d'oeuvres. George reached out and grabbed one. Since the guests were buzzed, he felt safe to let loose a little. He allowed himself to partake in a whiskey. Zane rested his hand on the deep contour of his secretary's back. He pointed to Sally and Gary Cooper with his left hand. He pointed to William Howard and his crew with his right.

"We'll film our journey and use the footage. He swung his arm and pointed to Kay melodramatically. "You, too! An Indian, disavowed by her tribe. A young couple stranded in the wilderness. The Indian saves them from a band of outlaws."

"How is this any different from your other stories, Zane?" Howard laughed, and the others followed the lead.

Zane was unperturbed. His voice slurred. "Why, this time, the Indian is a female. We'll let—what's your name?

Kay opened her mouth to speak but decided against answering.

"She will be the heroine of our film. That's how it will be different."

Sally gently pushed Gary away, who was breathing in her ear. She looked over at Kay and puffed, but the room was too loud for anyone to notice. George was relieved she had the good sense to be quiet.

Someone pointed to George. "What about the sentry guard over there? Who in the hell is that guy, anyway?"

Zane leaned forward from his waist and peered at him. "I thought he was one of William Clark's art pieces, a statue, from his antique collection." Laughter again.

In good spirit, Zane grinned and raised his glass. "What the hell! We'll bring the silent sentry along as protection. Okay with you? What's your name?"

Connie answered. "It's George. He'll go because I insist. As a chaperone. My daughter Sally is a young lady."

Zane opened his arms wide and faced Sally and Gary Cooper. "I doubt that, Mrs. Vandenberg, but she's a natural for the pictures, and don't those two look like they were favored with a kiss by the gods? Truly, what a handsome pair!"

They decided they would begin the adventure in four days. They retreated indoors to discuss the details. The plan was to ride by horseback early in the morning and aim for the canyon floor by noon, where it would be cooler by the creeks and under the trees. They would ride out late afternoon and break for camp where there was enough space for them all. Connie talked to Clark, Jr. while Sally and Gary Cooper talked to William Howard. Kay listened as Zane Grey pitched his story to her. The heat in the room gave George a headache. He did something uncustomary. He left his post. He jumped into the coupe and headed back up to Jerome. It was still early, and he wanted to see *Dr. Mabuse: The Gambler.*

He parked and went to the theater. He found a seat toward the front by the aisle. The plot of the film unfolded. In the dark, he smiled uncontrollably. Wow! There were the cobble streets, the asymmetrical buildings. He tried to remember the set designs and strained to find his face. He couldn't find himself in the crowd scenes. Then came the gambling scene. There! Standing in the corner in a tux looking square-jawed as he watched the gamblers. There he was in the riotous scene. He remembered he had been so high, he was surprised to see he managed to convey an emotion. All that makeup they had worn to create the garish smiles. What a dark film. What an awesome film. He had the urge to reach out to the people to his right and say, *Hey! Look, there I am.*

When the credits rolled, he looked for his name and saw in the middle of a long list, George Hero. He felt smug and proud. He stood, left the theater, and wandered about in the dark, watching the miners head to the nearest hooch. He stood at street corners, smoking cigarettes, breathing in the cool air and enjoying the vibe of the town. Two female hookers passed him and smiled. They were attractive enough.

"Come with us, mister! We will take good care of you."

He pulled out a flask of concentrated opium tea and guzzled it down. He followed them, attracted to one with the blonde hair. The night enveloped them as they walked arm in arm up the asymmetrical cobbled streets. He felt like he had jumped into Fritz Lang's film. The girls waved red scarves as they walked. He let the pair lead him to a hotel and up to the second floor. He entered the bedroom as the opium tea kicked in. He descended into a luxurious state of being as he plopped down on the mattress. They undressed him and covered him with their bodies. The opium tea blurred his vision, but his senses were heightened by the attention of the women. George had the impression they had turned into vampires. It must be the movie. What he wanted was to fall into the darkness and cease feeling.

CHAPTER FIVE

SALLY

Sally sat on a tall, blonde horse next to the others on the plateau and tried not to show her nervousness. It was late June, a week after the party. She had little experience riding a horse or the desire to explore the wilderness. However, Sally learned from her mother that it was the associations you made that got your foot in the door, not your talent. She wouldn't miss the chance to be around a gathering of men who might open the door wide. William Howard because she hoped he'd cut her a break and put her in a future picture. The cinematographer, Lucien Andriot, was excited to film footage for a future endeavor. Jack Holtz was an established star in the Westerns. Zane Grey was a famous writer whose stories were made into movies. Billy Clark because he was filthy rich and his friends were powerful people. Finally, she was sweet on Gary Cooper. His face was soft to the touch and his eyes dreamy. His goals for movie stardom matched her own. She saw them as a dynamic couple where maybe they could help each other rise to stardom. She wanted to kiss him, to mean something to him. But if not, at least he was good-looking and more fun to flirt with than the other men.

William Howard had picked her a gentle mare named Marigold, and as the horse stood there calmly waiting, Sally relaxed a bit and allowed the excitement of anticipation to fill her insides. The other riders were lively because they faced a breathtaking view, but for her, she saw opportunity. She was eighteen and beautiful. Someone would bend her way. She was certain of it.

They were on the top of a ridge looking north across the valley at bluffs layered with red sandstone, limestone, and siltstone. To get there would take all morning. They'd gradually descend across exposed flat land, through juniper and creosote bushes, and around a solitary hill which Zane Grey said was a volcanic deposit, but to Sally, the hill made her think of a chocolate Hershey's Kiss. They all agreed to this early start with the plan of reaching Sycamore Point by the end of to-morrow and at the cabin of Mayhew Lodge by the third day. Zane Grey had done this several years earlier and recounted memories of vertical cliffs following a winding creek. Sally remembered him weak at the knees at the party, describing his plan to revisit "hallowed ground." It was simple for him to persuade the others that the canyon was an easy trip to maneuver through and that Sally would be quite safe and not the only female in attendance. Connie consented, provided Kay and George went along. Sally would have gone without her blessing, and they both knew it. Sally pretended to oblige, and she agreed to the conditions simply because she was afraid her mother would make a scene in front of the men and ruin their impressions of her. Howard, Grey, and Clark agreed to split the cost to return the group to Clarkdale by cars and the horses by wooden trailers. Billy was flying back in his plane. He told Connie he'd bring Sally back by air and nudged her, whispering, "The view from the sky is a trip in itself. You'll love it up there, Sally. It beats the view from a car or the back of a horse any day."

Sally tried hard to retain her composure. "Up there? Oh, you bet, Billy. Count me in."

She knew it was a gentlemen's outing, and though they would be roughing it for a few days, she was happy to be included in the men's inner circle and thanked Kay in her mind. If she hadn't been invited in the first place to participate in *The Thundering Herd,* Sally would have missed this golden chance to wiggle her way into the motion picture industry. She found it strange that Kay did not seem the least bit interested in the picture. She was more concerned about acting as an Indian out in the wilderness.

Last night she discovered Kay in the field behind the barn. She had lit a small fire and sat on her knees. She had the bundled sage the Apache woman had given her and was fanning the smelly smoke, coating herself. When Sally asked Kay what she was doing, Kay replied with her eyes closed, "Cleansing myself for the journey."

"That stuff stinks."

"Then go back to the house, Sally."

The next morning, they sat in their horses and stood in a line and looked out at a gentle slope. The sun was rising. They drank coffee and ate a sweet roll served by the Mexican named Jesus, whom they hired to set up camp and cook for them. His wife cleaned a few of the engineers' homes, and Jesus was a regular cook for the Clark family. Jesus brought his dog, a short-haired mutt with long legs and a small body and an even smaller head. It didn't look like any breed at all. But it was happy enough, judging by the spotty-toothed grin and a tail that wagged constantly. Gary Cooper delivered coffee to Sally personally, and his attention made her pulse quicken.

Sally looked to Kay at her left and observed a rare smile. She was looking in her notebook. Sally leaned over to take a look. There were drawings of bushes and scribbled words.

"What's that?"

"Dahteste is teaching me about the plants of the desert. I have a list to find and bring back."

"That old lady that works on the farm?"

Kay nodded. "Her son and grandson come a few days a week to help." A pause. "I still don't know what's going to happen to them."

Sally watched Kay's smile disappear. Who knew what would happen? Sally learned recently that Connie didn't own the property. Billy was in charge. All Sally knew about the grandson of the Copper King was that he had celebrated his thirty-second birthday. He liked to fly planes. He was married and had two little children she had never seen. Kay was out of luck about owning the farm. She shied from telling Kay and felt a smidgen of remorse for suggesting she could solve her situation.

Sally looked to the right and smiled cordially at Zane Grey's secretary, who was in charge of typing up his notes when they returned. Sally wondered if she did more than take notes and hazarded a guess as to where she'd be sleeping. She supposed the men had arranged for her and Kay and Miss Whoever to share a tent.

Next to Grey was the movie team. Jack Holt laughed at something William Howard said. Lucien Andriot, looked through a type of periscope that Sally assumed judged the distance and light. He had spools of film packed in leather bags and two movie cameras sprawled on the back of a burro. He was ready to capture landscape shots for a future project. Gary Cooper and Billy had warmed to each other at the party. Billy decided to include him because Cooper was athletic and shared his enthusiasm for outdoor adventure. Billy brought a saddlebag full of gadgets. He fiddled with his black and gold Leitz Elmar camera, wiped the lens of his binoculars, and wiggled a blade on his Swiss Army knife as if he were a boy scout trying to earn a badge. And George. Connie had insisted that George join the group to protect Sally. *Good grief, she never lets up on the smothering act.* Sally was secretly pleased that George looked uncomfortable on his appointed horse which was too small for him. His long legs almost touched the ground. His grimace suggested his desire to explore the wilderness was nil.

The men wore blue jeans and bandanas. Some carried revolvers in holsters while Grey brought a shotgun. They all wore cowboy hats to block the sun. Sally felt like she was playing a part in a Western, a sequel to the bit part she stepped into in *The Thundering Herd*. This time her part was bigger, and she relished the trip, even though she disliked the desert. She looked down the hill below her at the scattered, scraggly bushes and dusty earth. With a "Yee-haw!" from Jack Holtz, it was time to begin. She and Kay were at the rear of the line, in front of Jesus, who rode a pony and pulled a burro behind him bearing kitchen gear and food supplies. The mutt barked while it ran up and down the line of excursionists on horseback.

What a motley crew of ten. She was told there would be time for relaxing at dusk. During the morning, they would ride and break for lunch where appropriate. They reiterated the plan to ride early out in the open, and during the hottest time of the day, descend to the canyon floor where it would be cooler by the creeks and the trees. They would ride out by late afternoon and make camp under the stars. Sally listed the possible dangers in her head. She figured the only real danger they faced would be if they were caught in a monsoon or if a mountain lion crossed their path. More likely, the only predator they would see would be a coyote. They would watch for partridges, quails, antelope, or mule deer. In that case, the men had assured her, they'd have a fine supper. What about those pig-like javelinas? She had seen the black wild things on the farm by the river, and the big male ones had tusks. Kay told her one had gored the Weeses' dog a few years back. Sally wasn't sure if Kay was teasing, but she put the javelina in the "beware" column in her mind. Kay said they were stupid creatures, blind and easy to scare away if you made some noise. Sally figured the noise the ten of them made would skitter away any possible threats. Monsoon. The flooding of the gushing rainwater could knock you down and swallow you up, Kay had told her. It was June and early for Monsoon season, so their chances favored no such torrential downpours. Then Kay warned her about the rattlesnakes waiting to strike an exposed ankle. And tarantulas. They might crawl into the tents. Sally put her hand over her pistol in her holster. She didn't know how to shoot it, but she'd be willing to learn on a tarantula. Damn Kay for trying to scare her. She wanted to smack off that smile she wore. *God, she likes it out here.* Sally sighed and tried to focus. Gary. Jack. Mr. Howard. Zane. Mr. Andriot. How best to get their attention?

They headed east toward the red sandstone bluffs in front of them. By noon, the band had ridden ten miles and appreciated the breeze at the high walled entrance of the canyon. The wind tunnel traveled through the crags and rubble. The brilliance of the sunlight had them all searching for shade. Kay pointed at the red layered walls and shouted, "Hey!" to the others. She got off her horse and hiked up to the large black circle in the sandstone layer that signified there was a cave. The group stopped and watched her climb, shielding their eyes from the sun. She sidestepped the sage bush and avoided the barrel cactus, with its yellow needles that threatened to poke her. George was the first to follow her. Zane Grey, Billy Clark, and Jack Holt hiked up after Kay disappeared inside. William Howard chatted with Grey's secretary. She seemed to be unaffected by the heat or inconveniences of the desert. Sally waited in front of boulders the size of a house which provided some shade. A roadrunner scurried by, his long tail feathers pointing straight behind him, his scrawny legs pushing him forward. It scrambled over the red, white, and black round rocks that looked like dinosaur eggs and disappeared. Grey's head emerged from the dark entrance.

"Ha! There are petroglyphs on the walls!"

Jesus the cook steered his burro into the shade left by an outcrop of junipers. He began fixing lunch. Sally let Gary Cooper lift her off Marigold. His smile created dimples on his cheeks, and his eyes flickered with emotion as he bent and kissed her cheek. Sally felt stiff, and her buttocks ached. She kept her complaints to herself, choosing instead to squeeze his hand and summon up a radiant smile that she hoped would woo him. She followed him up the hill. His lower back was wet with sweat. His jeans cupped his backside and his thighs were taut and muscular. Sally took a deep breath and exhaled quietly. Last week on the movie set, she discovered he was ten years older than she. She thought it was a good sign. He had more experience, and she knew when the time came, she would lose her virginity to Coop. She was a quick learner, and she would keep up with him. Her mother had taught her never to put out without getting something in return.

It was perplexing to admit, but Sally was reluctant to have sex with a man. All it seemed to do was ruin friendships. The lopsidedness of feelings between a pair surfaced and brought sadness. She understood intuitively her imaginings of a man and his capacity for love was superior to the reality. It was a vulnerable state of being to be attached to someone physically and emotionally. Couples rarely remained happy—just look at her parents. But, as she watched Coop's biceps flex under his shirt, Sally decided she would be willing to take a chance with Gary Cooper.

At the lip of the cave, Sally walked over to a huge window-like hole on the side wall that framed the view from where they had come. She took in the open valley and tried to retrace their steps with her eyes. The plateau seemed far away, a purple stripe on the horizon. Behind it, Mingus Mountain pierced the sunny haze and was majestic as a backdrop. She heard a grinding sound and looked below her. Lucien Andriot was filming her, rolling the camera reel and hiding behind a piece of dark cloth. Her heart leaped, and she struck a pose she hoped looked natural.

"You're fetching, Sally." She turned. Billy's camera shutter clicked. She gave him a half-smile and stepped into the interior of the cave, pleased with the attention. After her eyes adjusted, she observed the room was a half-circle with the mouth facing southeast. The sun overhead would travel behind the entrance, and the cave would remain cool for most of the day. The floor was wide and flat, and the walls smooth as Sally ran her hand over the pits and shiny levels of the surface. She made her way to where the men speculated and pointed at antelopes and snakes and red handprints painted on the walls. A man walked with a spear slung over his shoulder. They all contributed at once, united with awe.

"I'd say around one thousand A.D."

"Perfectly preserved."

"What'd you say they were?"

"Sinagua. Ancestors to the Hopi. They migrated in and out of this valley over a thousand years ago."

"A clan living right here up high where they were protected from the heat and animals."

"Farmers?"

"Yes, farmers. Usually they lived by the water. There's probably a creek nearby."

"Fascinating."

Sally stood by Kay who was busy drawing the patterns in her notebook. She concentrated on the shape of the room and drew that, too. Billy came over with his shiny camera and offered to share the pictures when his roll was developed. Kay thanked him and explored outside of the cave on a balcony ledge two feet wide that porched the bluff. The group had agreed no one was to wander off alone. George signaled he'd follow her. Billy snapped pictures of everyone in front of the glyphs.

They ate burritos made by Jesus, stretched their legs, and relaxed for an hour. The horses drank from a creek found around the corner from the cave. Sally positioned herself next to Coop. She remembered he mentioned going to school in England and inquired.

"My folks are English, and while Dad loved the rancher life and eventually became a hotshot judge in Montana, my very proper mother thought Montana was uncivilized. She shipped my brother and me to an English school. That didn't last too long, thank God. A few years is all. I hated it." He took a deep breath. "I find the western space and unending skies far more suitable."

Sally kept her hat low so that only her lips showed beneath the shade cast on her face. She refused to go without lipstick, reapplying a blush of pink to protect them. Sally recalled Kay's expression earlier when she shook her head with incredulity as Sally opened her compact mirror and pulled out her tube of lipstick from a pocket on her blouse. Kay walked past her with eyebrows arched while she put on her calfskin gloves and pulled out a knife. Sally watched Kay approach an unusual cactus, tall with many spindly, thorny arms. She consulted her notebook and recorded the plant. Then she cut off a limb and put a piece of it in her canvas satchel. With frustration, Sally turned away from Kay. *Must I forgo all femininity? Am I not wearing a cowboy hat? Baggy gauchos? A white shirt drooping past my shoulders, making my waist look bulky? Do I not smell from the heat and endure Marigold, who farts and brings about the flies? For Pete's sake, my lips will be pretty.*

Gary Cooper sat at ease in his saddle. He leaned down and grabbed her arm. He pushed back the cuff of her shirt and kissed the soft skin exposed at her wrist. When an accompanying breeze slid over her sweaty neck, her nipples puckered. He was a virile man. Sally marveled how the negative aspects of the desert disappeared when he was near.

Sally stepped in her stirrup and mounted Marigold. She watched Kay squat next to a different cactus. This one had blooming fuchsia-colored flowers. The silver-green paddles had black dots over them. George wandered over to Kay and instigated a conversation about what she discovered. She answered slowly, with an intentness that made George smile. Sally listened in on their conversation.

"I'm learning. According to Dahteste's drawing, this is a beaver cactus. I can take these paddles and pulverize it into a poultice to use on cuts and relieve pain. I can take the seeds inside and grind them up with water to make a mush and apply as a poultice to help heal cuts."

George tipped his hat back to reveal his face. The mole under his eye disappeared in the flash of the sunshine. "You told me you didn't like the woman."

"She has a way of seeping into your system. She means well."

He pointed to a cactus that was like the one she had severed earlier with the long, spindly arms. "What is this? I saw you cataloging it in your book."

Kay put the beaver cactus paddle into her bag and stood. She squinted at the tall specimen. "That's an ocotillo. You can use it for everything. Food. Or stick an arm into the ground and it will take root and make a fence to keep out Jack rabbits. You can peel the bark and roast it. The juice inside applied to an injury will take away pain and reduce swelling."

Kay smiled at George, and Sally looked at her with curiosity. Kay unwrapped a branch of the creosote bush from her bag. "Remember this morning when we crossed the valley and these bushes surrounded us?" George nodded. Sally remembered them. They scratched her calves when Marigold got too close. Sally thought they were ugly bushes but didn't say anything. It was the first time Kay had a lot to say, and Sally was surprised.

"The creosote can get rid of chest colds by burning the bark and breathing in the vapor or by drying the leaves and grinding them into a powder. As a tea, it helps for cramping."

George asked if any of the plants she collected were harmful.

"They all are if you use too much at one time. That's the part I'm learning. How much is enough to help and not make the situation worse." She reached into her canvas bag and carefully pulled out a vine with green leaves and a large white flower pressed between tissue paper. "This is jimsonweed." Kay pushed back her hat which revealed her wide cheekbones. Her dark eyes petted the flower. "It's toxic and used by shamans. The right amount brings visions. It's very dangerous, though." She put away the poisonous plant. "Dahteste makes a paste and uses it for broken bones and swollen joints." She rolled on to the back on her horse. "But take too much, and it will kill you."

Sally wondered when George and Kay became so chummy.

The group marched on through the canyon floor. It was an enjoyable day, and the light breeze and Coop's smiles elevated her mood until she felt lightheaded. They climbed up to open ground late afternoon as planned and set up camp. Jesus made a stew while the day dimmed into evening. After supper, the three women assisted Jesus in the cleanup and went off to freshen up. It was twilight, and the planet Jupiter appeared first. Minutes later, Sally felt like she had blinked twice and the world turned pitch black, save for the wood fire in the center of camp. The men drank whiskey and smoked cigars. Sally turned away from the fire and looked up at the stars, so brilliant and close, she felt like she should tip her head to avoid bumping into them. Sally had never been so exhausted. Everything hurt. She opened the flap to the ladies' tent and crouched down on top of folded blankets thinking she didn't care if a tarantula came in the tent or not. She listened to the murmuring of the men around the campfire and fell quickly asleep.

It was late. Sally heard a rustling. Zane Grey's secretary left the tent and the canvas flap shut the coolness outside. Kay was softly snoring. Sally couldn't see a thing. She crawled to the entrance and felt her way outside. The Milky Way was a long white road above her. Sally secretly hoped Gary Cooper was waiting outside her tent to lure her out. She quickly squatted behind a bush and peed. All was quiet. Back in the tent, she nodded off to sleep while replaying their conversations.

The next day, Sally's stiffness was excruciating, but she refused to complain. Especially after observing Kay's gait was loose and perky. Sally's mood sank when her morning cup of coffee was given to her by Jesus instead of Coop. The air felt muggy instead of dry, and the energy surrounding the camp had taken on a sour countenance. Cooper wouldn't make eye contact with her and stayed engaged in conversations with the others. After breakfast, the group guided their horses on foot and followed an animal path down into a gorge that shaped a creek. The walls of rock towered around them. She felt like she was trapped in a beautiful cage. The creek bank was lush with green grass, and the sycamore trees murmured as a breeze moved through their leaves. The water glistened in the sun and polished the rocks on the creek bed. Sally felt annoyed that such a beautiful morning was wasted.

There was a definite shift in the personalities of the men. What on earth had they talked about around the fire last night? Zane Grey was sullen as he led the group along the creek. His secretary looked anxious. Gary Cooper talked nonstop to William Howard, and they fell back to the end of the line to discuss something privately. Billy mumbled to himself as he spent most of the morning adjusting the settings on his camera and shooting the trees, cacti, and the textures etched on the walls of the gorge. He did not take one picture of her. Jack Holtz and Andriot chatted quietly and ignored her.

Sally pretended Coop's sudden disregard for her did not sting. He had been enthusiastic and charming for the last two weeks. Why today did he act like she was a stranger? He had readjusted his focus from her to the director. She figured Gary was making his sales pitch to him, trying hard to convince Howard to give him a part in his next film. She was so deflated, a wave of panic filled the back of her throat and mottled her neck with a rash. She willed herself to remain calm and focused her attention to Kay and George, who contributed to the weirdness of the morning by their intimate, constant conversation. *What did that cook put in the stew?* She hoped someone would offer an explanation, but she would not start the gossip. Ten scenarios played out in her head and occupied her time as they traveled the whole day without incident. Eyes watched dark clouds blemish the blue sky. It seemed like everyone wanted to get out of the constrictive gorge. The word "monsoon" was used by the group with anxious inflection. They took turns pointing to an angry formation behind them. How odd, Sally thought, when a beautiful setting could feel downright cursed.

Most felt it was necessary to make their ascent out of the gorge. Billy and William Howard looked at the map provided to them by the forestry department. Zane Grey huffed, "I've been here before. I am an expert in these parts, having made many trips like these over the past twenty years. Will you stop brooding? The monsoon season has barely begun."

Billy and William Howard looked doubtful.

Zane pulled the reins hard and faced them. "There is a pass a mile around the next bend where the horses can climb out safely."

Sally hoped it would be effortless to climb out of the restrictive passage. Yesterday's trek out of the gorge was scary. If Marigold had a misstep, well, she tried hard not to think about how far down she'd fall. She had touched the rock wall as they made their way out. She could not restrain herself from playing out catastrophic scenarios in her mind. She had turned her head and caught the blinking eye of Jesus's burro. It had the hardest job, carrying too many supplies on its back, yet it seemed to stay balanced on the narrow trail. Sally imagined it plunging to its death, braying, while the pots and pans and cans of food ricocheted off the slabs of rock.

Now she heard in the distance the rumbling of thunder and witnessed the congregation of clouds form into a slate curtain and dump rain somewhere behind them. Kay rode up next to Sally and studied her face. She said in a low voice, "Don't worry, it's far away." Sally made eye contact, inspected her relaxed mouth and calm eyes, and believed her. She was suddenly thankful Kay was next to her.

Lucien Andriot and Jack Holtz were the only two in the group who were excited. Holtz grabbed the movie camera that was tied to the back of Andriot's burro and passed it to him. Jack led the horse while Lucien turned backwards in his saddle and filmed the storm behind them. Jack held the horse steady. The dark-haired Frenchman bent his head in close to the projector lens. The cinematographer turned the crank and giggled. He whistled with enthusiasm.

"Quels nuages fantastiques. Je dois les capturer."

At the front of the line, Sally heard Billy concede to Zane. "I agree, we push ahead. Almost there, right? Who knows where that storm is heading?"

Zane answered with distaste, "You will feel better once we are up on higher ground."

The wind blew in gusts and Sally shivered, depressed. Where once Gary Cooper had made certain she was near, now he had positioned himself up at the front of the line far away from her. She was relegated to the back with Jesus, Kay, and George. Kay stopped suddenly and leaped off her horse to cut a piece of a new plant. The wind grabbed her cowboy hat and blew it across the other side of the creek. They would not stop to let her retrieve it. Jesus rode up to her. He reached in a sack and pulled out a spare hat. "Take it, miss. It's best to keep the sun out of your eyes. This storm will turn and we'll all be sweating in an hour. Take it."

Kay thanked him. She pulled her hair back and twisted it into a single braid that fell between her shoulders. Then she put the cap on. It was an old soldier's cap, black with an indecipherable label on the front. It was too big for her, and the bill of the cap fell to the top of her eyebrows. Sally thought Kay looked absurd. They found the uphill trail where the gorge met Oak Creek Canyon and formed a pass, just as Zane Grey predicted. They made their ascent.

Sally heard birds squawk and fly out of the trees.

The roar announced the water first, then around the bend behind them, the creek became a river, an orange-colored mess, as trunks of trees and harsh water slapped against the boulders. Sally's heart raced, and she swatted Marigold to hurry up the path. At a fork, the men went right, but Marigold spooked and veered left. Sally whimpered. There was no stopping the horse. Sally held on to Marigold's neck and closed her eyes and let Marigold take her where she wanted. The roar of the water below drowned out the sound of Sally's cries. She didn't know if Kay or George or the cook had followed her, or if they went right with the others. She was too terrified to look. Whatever trail there had been was now a dead end. Marigold whinnied, unsure where to step. Marigold made her way through the rocks, stepping on the dirt, while her belly and Sally's legs pressed up against the rock face. Sally held her breath and tried her best to lay on Marigold's back and not move. A few minutes later, Marigold stopped. The sound of the monsoon river decreased from roar to rumble. Sally took a deep breath and sat up. Behind her, she saw Kay's black cap and George following at the rear. The three of them were separated from the group. They were high up, out of danger of the wash, but stuck on a ledge with an overhang. It might have been used as a cave at one time, but now it was nothing more than a flat plate and slight cover from the rain.

Kay got down off her horse. George barked at her, "Sally, what were you thinking? We have to go back and get on the trail with the others."

"Marigold wanted to come this way."

Kay spit. "You have to tell the horse where to go. Now look at us!"

George's horse walked to the edge of the table rock formation. His flank was cut. George's left elbow was bleeding badly. White bone poked up in the air.

Sally squealed and covered her mouth to swallow down reflux bile. "Jesus, George, that's a nasty break."

"Pipe down and help me off this horse."

Kay peered through the rain and caught sight of the group a far distance up on the ridge. She whistled loudly as if calling for Marvin in the back pasture and waved her black cap until they saw her. She tied her red bandana on a branch by the ledge so they would not lose sight of them. Then she pulled off her horse the canvas bag of collected plants and cacti.

"Are you sure you know what you're doing?" George asked as he dropped to his knees.

She put her cap back on. The lip fell low over her face, but it kept the rain out of her eyes. Kay squatted next to George. He moaned and grimaced at the bone poking through his shirt. Blood dripped out of his ear. He started panting.

"Give me something! I know you have magic in that bag of yours."

Sally watched Kay bite her lower lip and shake her head with worry. She reached in the bag and pulled out the jimsonweed. "Enough will dull your pain."

She got her canteen and her pestle and mortar. He started to panic, so she added more water and pounded quickly. He opened his eyes and stared at Kay with confusion. She leaned against him and his agitation grew ferocious.

"Where are my emeralds? I know you have them. Do you have them now?" He smacked her with the stub of his right arm, and it almost knocked her over. "Where are they?"

"Right here, George. I got 'em. Drink this first. Settle down."

Sally watched Kay give him her potion. He gasped and drank it. Kay wrapped his elbow as best she could, but they were covered in mud, and Sally could feel Kay's frustration. Time passed.

The wind redirected the clouds over the red rock plate that held them. Lightning crackled, and Marigold ran away. The sky grew dark, and the diffused light of the day created shadows over their faces. George stared at Kay and shook his head with disbelief. He reached out and tried to touch Kay's face. His throat gurgled while he blinked at her. George exhaled grandly and a resigned look registered on his features.

Under the overhang, the rain dumped from the sky, and the spray hit Sally like needles. She held onto the two remaining horses and pulled them under the overhang as much as possible. Sally told the creatures it would be okay. She grabbed a blanket off of Kay's horse and wrapped it around herself. She lowered herself and sat on a rock. It was uncomfortable, but better than getting soaked and muddy on the ground. Looking at Kay and George a few feet from her, she could hardly hear what they said over the downpour.

Sally decided to push for answers. She asked George what went wrong with everyone last night. He squinted at her. With erratic breathing he told her that Grey and Howard fought over Paramount Studios. Howard was instructed to alter the script adaptation from Grey's book. Howard told him that Paramount wasn't interested in Zane Grey westerns anymore. Then Grey caught his secretary necking with Jack Holtz. Zane cried it was all a conspiracy to sabotage his career. "I gave Grey the rest of my tea. It helped him calm down and go to sleep." George chuckled. "The man can't handle his whiskey, is all." Sally wondered if he was delirious. She was greedy to know more. George looked at Sally and convulsed with laughter. She had never heard him like this. The pitch of his voice was deep and soulful.

He announced loudly to her, "Howard asked me to be in his next film. How about that, little Sheba? Not you. Not Cooper. But me."

Sally stepped backward as if punched. George Hero squinted at Kay wearing the military hat. "Private Cox? Is that you? Where are the emeralds? Is the pistol still in the box in the barn?"

Kay's voice quavered. "Yes."

George swallowed hard. "What are you gonna do with them?"

Kay spoke calmly. "There's a new school at Flagstaff. Northern Arizona University. They let women in, even Indians. I thought about learning finances. I want my own farm. Milking cows. Maybe an orchard."

George's body slackened. His eyes rolled out to catch the view from their perch. He shifted his head and tried to focus on Kay, but he saw someone else.

"Cox, go to Los Angeles. There's a man I know. Eugene Baxter.

He'll give you cash for the emeralds. That was my plan. I was going to disappear. But your idea of a farm"—he spasmed hard with cramps. "Aim higher."

He closed his eyes.

Sally looked at Kay. "What did he say about the emeralds?"

They stared at each other. George groaned and hit Kay in the shoulder with his stub.

"Private Cox?"

Kay rubbed his forehead with her thumb. "Yes."

"Give me more of your magic. I want to sleep."

She pulverized more jimsonweed.

He looked at the rain falling down from the Arizona sky. Something occurred to him. He swung his head to Private Cox and hit Kay again.

"Do you think I'll see Mitzi?"

Sally watched Kay rub the rain off his cheeks. She gently closed his eyes. "Sure, George."

"More. I need more."

Kay pounded up the rest of the jimsonweed, added water from her canteen, and gave the toxin to him. She held him while he shook. The blood from the elbow break trailed away in a stream and mixed with the rain. It fell off the ledge like a slender waterfall.

Sally watched them both. Was it tears or rain on Kay's face?

Then he was still.

Kay stood up slowly and walked over to the entrance to check if she could see the others. Sally walked over to George. She stood over him and watched the rain drops jump off his cheek. The mole under his eye was dark like a polka dot. It triggered the time she had joined him in Saint Louis. She was on her way back to Connie in Chicago to pick up her things. She had met her Aunt Bernice and the three of them decided she could live in Jerome for one year. George was told to escort her home. He met her in St. Louis. He was plastered. He manhandled her all the way back to the hotel, threatening her and poking her with a hairpin until he finally passed out in his chair. The six-hour ride was horrifying for Sally. She marched to her mother's room and demanded she do something. She laughed.

George's eyes stared out like blue glass. Sally took her boot and pushed him over the cliff ledge into the canyon.

Kay turned, and with an abrupt intake of breath cried, "Why?"

* * *

William Clark III had a powder blue De Havilland Gipsy Moth with two seats. Billy made good on his word and helped Sally into the back seat of the plane. He gave her a pair of aviator glasses, cotton balls for her ears, and a blanket for her lap. The sun would be up soon to start another day. "It will be cold up there. But wait until you see the sunrise!"

Sally realized she clenched her whole body. She settled in the seat behind Billy. He bragged that his friend Jack Lynch, the former instructor of Charles Lindberg, had trained him. Lynch had been teaching him how to fly blind by covering his cockpit. It was he who had flown the plane from Cottonwood to Sedona. Now it was dawn, the sky was clear, and Billy looked through the windshield as he rolled down a dirt road next to the Mayhew Lodge while Lynch gave him a two-finger salute. The plane lifted off the ground, and Sally leaned back with diverse emotions; she was breathless with the liftoff and her topside view and the gripping exhaustion that urged her eyes to sleep. As she gaped at the beautiful red rock formations that Billy flew around, he ascended in altitude. She looked down to see the line of Model Ts and trucks below, which were taking the expedition party, the horses, and the burros back to Cottonwood. She recollected the last twenty-four hours and groaned heavily. After Kay and she were rescued off the ledge, the rain stopped and they walked around the bulging discs of the canyon. Zane Grey announced they were in Oak Creek Canyon, and in a few miles they'd make it out and arrive at Mayhew Lodge.

The group was solemn. Kay didn't speak to Sally but sat stone-faced on her horse. Sally was forced to ride Jesus's burro since Marigold had run away and no one could find her. They discovered her two miles later. She squealed at quick, repetitive intervals. Her ankle was trapped between two large rocks. Sally retched when Jack Holtz shot Marigold behind the head. The group was silent as Grey led them cautiously through the canyon until they faced the L-shaped, log-chinked lodge with dormers and cedar shake awnings. A thick rock chimney and rock fence surrounded the front yard. They stayed at the Mayhew Lodge overnight, courtesy of Billy. He used their phone and made arrangements for the transfer back to Cottonwood. He called the police. They said they'd work on getting a team of volunteers to retrieve George Hero's body. Sally took a hot bath in the upstairs bathroom, not caring that Kay and Mr. Grey's secretary were waiting. She wept in her washcloth as quietly as she could. She pulled the plain, clean blanket up to her chin. In her mind, she watched George fall like a leaf to the rocks below. The thought of how her mother would take the news briefly entered her thoughts, and she pushed them away. She didn't want to analyze the disappointments. Gary Cooper had kissed her hand goodbye when they emerged from Oak Creek Canyon. He told her he was riding in with the sheriff to Sedona. He wished her luck and gave her a dimpled smile and was gone. She was glad she had not lost her virginity to him. She let the numbness of her body and mind take over and slept.

Now she was in Billy's plane. The air was sweet with the smell of pine trees. The sunrise didn't disappoint. The peach splash on the eastern horizon took her breath away. She tapped Billy on the shoulder and thanked him loudly, although the sound of the propellers made her words impossible to hear. She looked down at Sedona's terracotta columns. Billy flew his plane easily between two gigantic posts of stacked red boulders. On the dirt road leading to Clarkdale, she saw people riding horses. She saw men driving Model Ts. And here she was in Billy's plane. It occurred to her what an unusual year 1928 was turning out to be. Encapsulated in a unique moment she saw the past, the present, and the future. She was experiencing it all, right now. She was eighteen. She would go to Hollywood with the letter of recommendation William Howard signed this morning over breakfast. One day, she would be a star. Bigger than Gary Cooper.

She was certain of it.

CHAPTER SIX

KAY

K ay repeated the name George had whispered to her before his heart stopped beating on the red rock ledge. It synched with the train rattling on the track. *Eugene Baxter. Eugene Baxter. Eugene Baxter.* She sat across from Mr. Vandenberg. Sally sat next to her. The San Pedro, Los Angeles, and Salt Lake Railroad belonged to William A. Clark's estate, and the three sat in the passenger car all to themselves, compliments of the grandson Billy Clark. The train headed to Clark's depot four hours away. Strategically placed to converge California shipping and Midwest markets, it was a spot on the floor of the Mojave Desert at the center of nowhere. The strip of the town rushed to be built. A bank. A mercantile store. A sheriff's office. A block of houses. And the Clark train depot. A new county was named in his honor, and the town was called Las Vegas.

The buoyant train matched their moods. The events of the last month unhitched propriety as the three attempted to make sense of recent events. They shared inner thoughts which a few weeks ago were unthinkable. Sally recalled how much she liked riding trains but then verbally smacked them with an unsettling declaration.

"Two years ago, I visited Aunt Bernice for the first time. On my return trip, I was in St. Louis and George met me there. We returned to Chicago together. He was three sheets to the wind and his hands were all over me." She cringed. "The weirdo gave me a hairpin and a box of chocolates and mumbled at my neck until he passed out at Springfield."

Jonathan Vandenberg's shocked expression froze on his face. "Sally, why didn't you say something?"

"Mother didn't believe me."

Kay wondered if this was Sally's need of attention. Kay thought of the milking cow back in Clarkdale. Sometimes it needed a sharp jab in the loin to instigate movement. This was Sally's tactic—to prod her parents in order to get a reaction. He looked at Sally and was at a loss for words. When he did not fawn with sympathy, Sally tried to hide her disappointment, but the tears slipped to her cheekbones. Jonathan gave her his white, ironed handkerchief. She blew hard into it. Was she crying wolf? Had George molested her? Kay sighed and bit her lip.

Kay offered the only logical explanation she could think of. "People have many sides to them, don't you think so? Some sides are for show-ing. Other sides are best kept hidden." She looked Jonathan in the eyes. "If I hadn't seen you at the farm, I wouldn't have met Sally or you or . . ."

Sally looked at Kay with disgust. "Did you have a crush on George Hero?"

Kay would not rise to the bait. It would injure their friendship. Somehow Sally was aware of the intimacies shared between George and herself, and it sickened Sally. How could she tell Sally that George had been kind to her and treated her as a desirable woman? Not some mutation of German parents and Hopi ghosts? George saw her as Kay and was interested in what she would become. After their initial con-summation at the Grand Hotel, they had met twice more and discovered they could talk freely with each other. They saw in themselves a mutual haven for communication. In short, they became friends. He shared with her his part in the Great War. He told her about Private Cox and Mitzi and how he had been in Fritz Lang's movie. He understood she was at a crossroads. She told him she was not sure whether to migrate to the Hopi Reservation east of Flagstaff or go to college. She was unsure what to do with her life. What about the animals at the farm? What about Daheste? She felt guilty for failing to keep them safe. George told her she would have to sever her ties with the farm and Dahteste. She had a responsibility to herself to figure out what to do next.

"There's no male in your life you could marry?" he had asked. Kay smiled and said she thought she had better stay single. She did not want to rely on anyone for support. Their budding friendship became precious to her. Kay almost told him about the emeralds but refrained. She suspected he wanted to ask, and she was glad he chose not to. It was a tacit feeling they shared. Theirs was a need for emotional intimacy, and the emeralds inside the gold-plated pistol would kill it.

As Kay thought about these things, she rubbed a piece of the soft fabric of Sally's skirt that brushed up against her blue cotton dress. How sudden and illogical the ways of the heart! Kay was caught in the irony as she understood that Sally had felt threatened by George while Kay longed for his companionship.

Mr. Vandenberg's expression became lively. He asked in a hushed tone to Sally, "Is that why you decided to cut your hair short and dye it black? I thought you were trying to look like Clara Bow. I do wish you'd go back to your natural color. You are beautiful as a blonde."

Sally considered her father. After a pause she said, "Maybe I will."

He looked out the train window and watched dry vacant land flash by the passenger car. Warming to his daughter, it was Jonathan's turn to muse. "I remember when I was a boy, my sister and I crossed half the country. We were sent from the orphanage in New York City to Illinois to live with farmers. They thought the fresh air would do us good." Jonathan half-smiled. "They called us orphan train riders. My sister was pretty like you, Sally. She had a fierce spirit. For years, I used to think Annette wanted to get away from me. When I grew older, I realized she wanted to be free to live her life without confinements. A lot of my sister is in you, my dear."

"Why is this the first time I'm hearing about her? It's all so ridiculous," Sally was exasperated. "I don't know you, Dad."

The train veered north rocking the three passengers at the end of the cargo line like the tail of a snake bumping over the cracked earth of the desert. A mountain range shimmered on the horizon and offered a change to an otherwise unremarkable view.

Jonathan regarded his daughter. "I think people will do just about anything to be rid of the restrictions placed on them by others." He took a deep breath and announced, "I'm divorcing your mother. I think about all the years I was too weak to stand up to her harsh disposition. I thought if I turned away and kept the peace, everything would be alright. I'm sorry, Sally."

He turned to Kay. "So you see, when you spend your life in hiding, overlooking the bad, hoping the ugly bits in people change in time—eventually, the ugliness becomes a natural state of affairs."

Kay asked, "George and Connie?"

"For years."

Kay wondered if it was joy or pain that lifted her brows and rounded her eyes? Sally whispered, "What did Connie say? Does she know you want to divorce?"

"Yes. That is partially why I'm escorting you to Los Angeles. I've agreed to a settlement, enough for me to live modestly." His eyes turned misty, and his smile was timid as he verbalized his plans. "I'm going to buy a bungalow by the ocean. I'm going to paint. I want to see you as much as you'll let me. Live with me if you want until you figure out your plans."

Sally sat back, stunned.

Jonathan cleared his throat. His cornflower eyes aimed at Kay. "Okay, what about you?"

Kay felt the overwhelming urge to unload the burden she was carrying. She felt charity emanating from Jonathan Vandenberg. She held her breath and reached for the holster strapped to her thigh and pulled out the gold-plated pistol, warm and shiny. She laid it in front of them. The swaying train made it dance on the table. Father and daughter leaned forward to look at the engraved leaves and acorns on the blonde grip, the intricate ribs, and geometric patterns carved on the barrel.

Kay spoke. "It was George's. He got it while he was in Germany. It meant a lot to him."

Sally said sarcastically, "I think what's inside the gun mattered to him more."

Jonathan put his elbows on the table and cupped his chin in his palm. "So, this is the reason why George shot me back at the farm? I didn't even know it was his."

Kay used her fingernail and carefully pulled open the lever on the butt of the pistol. She opened her palm and forty emeralds fell into her palm. Minus the red beryl. It was Jonathan's turn to sit back, surprised.

Kay stirred them with her finger. "George got these from Connie. I don't know the circumstances surrounding how he got them. He obviously hid them. I assume he stole them. He told me on the ledge before he died to take the emeralds to Los Angeles and cash them in and keep the money. I have a man's name. And so that's what I'm going to do."

Jonathan and Sally didn't reply. Kay expected them to grab the emeralds or demand she turn them over. Instead, she put the gems back into the gun and re-holstered the pistol to her thigh. She looked out the window, wary of making eye contact. She slowly exhaled.

A few hours later they arrived at a cross junction in Nevada where few buildings stood. A side street showed construction activity. A population of immigrants and migrants stacked brick with mortar. Irish,

Chinese, Hispanics, and Negros cut timber, made sidewalks, and hoisted beams while their hammers were like dance partners making graceful arcs in the air. The Clark train came to a slow stop. The train to Los Angeles would arrive in an hour. There was running water and a toilet at the depot. They waited in the lobby and sat under a fan, which stirred hot air. Kay had been waiting for Sally to say something. It took her almost two hours to finally say what was on her mind.

"I think once you cash in those emeralds, you ought to split the money three ways."

* * *

Kay stepped inside the pawn shop belonging to Eugene Baxter. She held her breath as she explained her connection to George Hero. After a few questions, he asked to look at the emeralds. She emptied them onto velvet material on the glass countertop. He held a few up to the light and smiled. "I don't know how you got these and I don't want to know." He pulled out a tiny paper bag and suggested she should put the emeralds into the bag while he cut her check for 500 dollars. "I will have to find a buyer and charge you a commission fee. Come back next week."

Kay wasn't sure what she should do. She started to put the emeralds back into the pistol.

"You want to unload the pistol?"

Kay surprised herself by answering quickly, "No. It's not for sale."

Eugene Baxter hid behind thick glasses and shrugged. "Leave me a few of those as collateral. I have to check their authenticity with a friend I know across town. You hold on to the check. We'll make a deal next week, okay, Injun?"

Kay's anger ignited. "My name is Kay Weese. Kay is Hopi for 'sister.' Weese is a German variation for 'white.' I'm a blend of both, you see?" Just as suddenly, her anger was doused by a realization. She relaxed her clenched jaw. She understood. *Like the red beryl in my pocket, my impurities make me different but also very rare. So be it.*

Eugene Baxter bowed with mock sincerity. "Yes, of course, Miss Weese."

She left a few green emeralds, grabbed the pistol, and with the 500-dollar check, agreed to return in a week.

* * *

To bind the three of them in the secret, Kay decided to split the money at the expense of Connie Vandenberg. Jonathan and Sally let her make the arrangements to sell the emeralds. All three rationalized that Connie had stolen a lot from them. George his life. Kay her home. Jonathan his marriage. Sally her childhood. They knew it was a cop-out. How easy to blame their weaknesses on Connie's dominating personality. Regardless, it justified their position and filled them with a false courage, which made it easier to cash in the jewels and take the money. Moreover, Connie wasn't aware the emeralds were missing. Apparently her surplus was such that they could get away with it. Cashing in the emeralds became the payoff for the pain. Kay couldn't part with the red beryl and did not tell the other two. Kay put the pink emerald inside the wooden box that held the kachina doll and feathers belonging to the mother and sister from her dreams. The red beryl felt far away and unsafe in the box, so she had the emerald set and attached to a long silver chain and wore it around her neck. She returned George's gold-plated pistol to Jonathan as compensation for George's shot into his shoulder at the farm.

Kay vowed to use the cash in a good way. She prayed to the Weeses' Christian God and to the Hopi's Great Spirit for guidance. Which one would hear and steer her to the right path? She still did not know what to do with her life.

On August 1, 1928, Kay split 66,000 dollars with Jonathan and Sally and said goodbye. Jonathan was in the process of buying a bungalow in Ocean Park just a block from the Pacific Ocean for 2,000 dollars. She did not like the many buildings and crowds of people in the downtown area. Sally said she had heard over a million people lived in Los Angeles. Kay declined the offer to stay with them and gravitated north to the outskirts of Los Angeles to find some breathing space. She enjoyed taking electric streetcars to explore her surroundings. One took her north, and she found herself at the end of a line at the Grand Central Air Terminal in the county of Glendale.

On the outside, she admired the two-story, Spanish-style terminal with a control tower five stories tall with blunt corners like a turret. She entered the building and wandered about the airy reception area containing benches for waiting, a ticket counter, and a coffee shop. She liked the colorful tiled floor and the fancy metal railings leading to the second floor. She recognized the moldings on the ceiling corners and lighting sconces were Art Deco. It was an elegant room. She climbed the stairs to the second floor and bypassed the entrance door to an upscale restaurant in favor of stepping out to the veranda. In the shade under the arches, Kay smiled broadly at the expansive views of the lined hangers butting to the wide runway with the long paved airstrip and the San Bernardino Hills as a backdrop. She decided to rent a room in the neighborhood and got in the habit of spending her mornings sitting at a small table on the veranda, skimming magazines and watching the planes take off and land.

Last week, Sally called the boarding house Kay lived in and arranged for them to meet at Bob's Big Boy diner, halfway between Glendale and the enterprising area called Hollywood. Sally rambled on about her experiences with Paramount and Metro-Goldwyn-Mayer.

"I dropped Zane Grey's name and showed them my letter from William Howard vouching for me. I got past the secretary but was surprised Mr. Zukor would not see me. He's the owner of Paramount Studios, you know."

Kay had little interest in the motion picture industry and only half listened to the buzz surrounding the new technology that synchronized voices to the images on the film reel. According to a magazine article in the *California Revue,* many predicted talkies would make the silent films obsolete. Marquees and billboards featured current stars like Rudolph Valentino and John Barrymore as well as upcoming stars like Joan Crawford and Janet Gaynor. Newspapers highlighted Douglas Fairbanks announcing his idea for a banquet to honor the best acting and best film of the year, calling it the Academy of Motion Pictures awards ceremony to be held in May of 1929. Kay's mind wandered to a moment last week when she was downtown and turned a corner and there was a giant-sized poster of Douglas Fairbanks and his son smiling at her. She immediately thought of Jonathan Vandenberg and wondered if she should suggest he pursue acting in the movies since he could be Junior's double.

Sally tilted her head to reclaim Kay's attention. "I had better success with the producer Mr. Schulberg. He was standing in the hallway of the house they use for meetings. I gave him a grand smile. Don't you know, it worked! I have an audition to dance for a part as a flapper in an upcoming musical." She sat back and sipped her coffee prettily. "It's only a matter of time. You wait, you'll see my name up on the marquee before 1928 is over."

Kay grabbed Sally's gloved hand. "Thank you."

Sally smirked. "For what?"

"For sharing that rooftop closet in Jerome with me that first night we met. I never knew anyone with more spunk than you, Sally Vandenberg."

Sally leaned over the table and pecked her cheek. Then she sat back and adjusted her bell-shaped hat. Sally had taken her father's advice and dyed her hair back to blonde. Kay thought Sally looked better and envied the determination that filled her eyes.

* * *

Kay mustered up the courage to wander over to the hangar and snoop around. She was unnoticed. She took a deep breath and went back to the airport to ask for a job from the company operating the airport, Curtiss Flying Service. The secretary knocked on the door of the manager and C.C. Moseley opened it. He said he had no work except for some janitorial shifts in the terminal. Kay thought for a brief moment.

"After my shift, can I volunteer at the hangars? Help clean the planes?"

The secretary looked at her disapprovingly, but C.C. Moseley studied her. "We'll see after a couple weeks. See if you fit in." He told the secretary to set her up for three days a week and pay her thirty-five cents an hour. Kay said she'd take the job.

During the month of August, Kay cleaned the bathrooms and swept and mopped the floors of the terminal. After a week, she repeated her request to C.C. Moseley to help at the hangars. He stifled his smile and gave her a gruff confirmation.

"Don't be a nuisance."

Slowly she got to know the mechanics and local pilots who flew in and out of the airport. Kay had a tendency to reach for the silver chain around her neck and rub the stone through her work shirt. The red beryl became her talisman.

In her spare time, Kay read the *Los Angeles Times* and discovered there was a large population of Indians living throughout the area. She read an article about the War Paint Club, Indians who advocated for labor rights in the film industry. Kay's eyebrows flew up when she learned they objected the use of hiring non-Indians to play Indian roles. She couldn't resist and took a streetcar to a large park where several tribes gathered and camped in clusters depending on the tribe. As long as they kept the noise down, the cops didn't make them leave the park for loitering. After finding a couple members of the War Paint Club, and telling them her experience on *The Thundering Herd,* they made her sign up. She asked them if there were Hopi in the park, and they pointed in the direction of a group of women who sat in a circle at the opposite end. Their laughter gave Kay the courage to approach them. Kay was relieved they welcomed her into their circle and told her to sit down. They agreed to teach her the way of the Hopi. As the days turned into weeks and 1928 was drawing to a close, Kay thought less in German and spoke actively in Hopi as best she could.

On a sunny, crisp day in December, Kay found her calling.

At the Grand Central Air Terminal, Kay stood at the edge of Hangar One and smiled at three women who came out to smoke. They were in the middle of a lively conversation and didn't seem to mind her presence. Kay thought of George who prided himself for his ability to stay hidden right in front of people, silently listening to all conversations. Kay stood tall and froze, looking up and away. Let them move if the conversation was private. They didn't. One woman was as tall as Kay with short brown hair and a wide mouth full of teeth. She called the shorter one next to her Muriel. During their chat, the third one was addressed as Louise Thaden. Kay listened to them discuss starting up a new organization and a magazine featuring women pilots.

Louise said, "The group on the east coast wants you to be the first president. With your approval, more girls will get their licenses. So far we have about fifty who have applied, but we are aiming for ninety-nine female pilots at the end of next year. We'd like to call the club the Ninety-Nines."

Amelia nodded. "It's time we organized and chronicle our progress,

I agree. The Ninety-Nines has a nice ring to it."

Muriel said, "You're on to something, Amelia. Since your hubby has finished booking your Midwest tour, you can promote the magazine and invite women to join the Ninety-Nines."

Amelia Earhart put up her hands as though to defend herself and laughed. She caught Kay's eye and waved her arms wide as though the Grand Central Air Terminal could be all hers. She pointed up to the sky.

"How about you? Wanna become a female pilot? We're gonna silence the bastards who say women don't have the smarts or the nerves to fly."

Muriel asked, "You look like an Indian. What's your tribe?"

"My Mother was Hopi. I was raised white."

Louise Thaden interjected, "What about that Indian from Oregon? What did she say she was? Chickasaw? Cheyenne? Now there's a tough group of women. Let's ask more American Indians to join."

Muriel asked Kay, "Are you afraid of heights?"

Kay thought of the time she climbed to a high ridge of Mingus Mountain and slept on the edge overlooking the entire Verde Valley. "No."

She remembered George's last words to her. *Aim higher.*

Amelia looked at Kay's push broom. "I will talk to Moseley. See if he will let you help us with the maintenance of the planes. If it interests you, we can try some lessons and get you up in the air to see if you like it."

Kay moved her thumb over the red beryl on her chest. *Aim higher.* She grinned. "Maybe I could buy my own plane and fly wherever I want, whenever I want."

They laughed. "Sure, sure."

"You could help us get the word out and help us recruit."

"Help us with the Ninety-Nines."

Kay's heart expanded. "You won't regret it."

CHAPTER SIX

* * *

Kay took well to flying. Throughout the first few months of 1929, she learned from various people at the airport including Earhart when she was around. She enrolled Kay in the piloting school which cost one dollar a lesson. Kay studied the parts of the plane and learned how to perform basic maintenance procedures. When she wasn't at the airport, Kay frequented the Hopi gathered at the park. She made friends with a girl named Kora, who was slightly older than Kay. Kora had two small children and a husband. One day, Kora twisted Kay's hair to signify she was a maiden of the Hopi. Two large circles like coiled black plates were pinned on the side of her head over her ears. Kay looked at herself in a department store window across from the Hopi camp and giggled. She adjusted her response so that Kora wasn't insulted.

It was fast, Kora's wooing. The clan wanted to leave the park and return to Arizona, to the third Mesa, northeast of Flagstaff, to the village of Bacavi. It was a reservation in the Old Oraibi. They wanted to return to the hills and Kora asked her incessantly to join them.

"We will find you a good husband. You will have children of your own. I can teach you more of the Hopi language. It's where you belong, with us."

Kay was tempted. Hadn't she daydreamed about her mother and sister for years? Kay gently patted her black hair twisted in two knots above her ears. Kora was affectionate. When Kay appeared, Kora made loud sounds and ran to her. She would hold Kay's arm or hand. Kay was not used to demonstrations and began to feel like she was held captive. In addition to Kora's possessive tendencies, Kora wouldn't stop daydreaming about their time together when they moved. Best friends. Sisters. The more Kora pushed, Kay realized it was her new friend who needed her more than the other way around. Eventually, Kay found ways to avoid visiting her. A month went by. Kay took a day off from her training and went to the park. When she saw the park was empty, she immediately felt guilty. What was wrong with her?

Then there was Sally. They continued to meet once a month at Bob's Big Boy diner. She shared the good news that Jonathan had settled in nicely in his two bedroom home. Sally occupied the guest bedroom and told her she would stay until her career took off. The separate garage was a good size with an attached room at the back of it with a commode and a sink.

"I told my dad to have Casper come out and live with us. I can't stand the thought of him alone at the hotel knowing my mother will kick him out to the streets. Then what would he do?"

Jonathan thought it was a great idea.

Sally proceeded with a progress report about herself. As the monthly meetings continued into the summer of 1929, her pretty smile disappeared. Nothing seemed to lift her mood, even when Kay told her she had earned her recreational pilot's license. Kay noticed Sally was buying Lucky Strikes in a box instead of rolling her own cigarettes. She puffed one after the other, tapping her cigarette on the table before lighting it, dramatically flicking the match out, and inhaling with gusto.

Kay flew constantly and expanded her boundaries. She figured sooner or later, those who suffered from the stock market crash from last October would part with a plane at a buyer's price. After patiently biding her time, Kay made a deal for a 1926 Stearman C-3B aircraft. She uncovered her split from the sale of the emeralds hidden in her room at the boarding house and paid 20,000 dollars for a used plane in fine shape. On its fuselage, U.S. Air Mail was sanded and removed. Kay decided to name her plane *Marvin* and had the letters painted in black. For Kay, up in the sky, she escaped the Depression. She was never happier.

A year went by.

Kay and Sally sat down in their corner booth at Bob's diner. She told Kay the bad news that since the October 29 crash, everyone was caught off guard, including Connie Vandenberg.

"Mother has visited me. She flies into Glendale Airport. Have you seen her? She insinuated that she needed to cash in her investments to recoup her losses." Sally inspected her painted nails. She casually continued, "She got out of her lease at the farm in Clarkdale. She got rid of the animals. She hinted that she wanted to cash in some of her precious jewels and noticed her emerald collection was missing."

Kay wanted to mourn the loss of the farm and Marvin. All she heard was the gentle threat of Connie invading her life about the stolen emeralds. She immediately pressed the red beryl hidden at her chest. "What did you say?"

"I told her the truth. That George stole them. Who knew what happened to them now that he was dead."

Kay winced at Sally's nonchalance. "Now what?"

"Nothing. We do nothing. I don't know about you, but I hid a big chunk of my share. My father, unfortunately, put his in the bank and lost most of it. What of you? What did you do with your split?"

Kay wasn't sure if she should tell her that she bought a used plane and named it *Marvin*. The rest was in a bag under a floorboard hidden in her room. She had two thousand dollars.

A feeling of dread filled Kay. She tried to divert the conversation back to Sally. "Any luck starring in movie pictures?"

Sally looked over Kay's shoulder with a bemused expression. "No luck landing a part, but I became friends with a dancer named Vasso at an audition. God, she's good. But even better is her brother, Hermes. They're Greek and starred on Broadway. They are giving it a go in Hollywood. Vasso Pan convinced me to be an assistant choreographer with her and learn from her brother. There are both involved in an upcoming film at RKO starring Ginger Rogers and Fred Astaire. It pays pennies, but you never know, I could run into Howard Hughes and just like that," she snapped her fingers, "I'm the new 'it' girl."

"Have you met any other movie stars?"

"I went to a New Year's party with Vasso, and I saw Rod La Rocque and Barbara Stanwyck promoting their new film." She sighed with disappointment. "The biggest celebrity I've met is Joan Crawford. I shook her hand. They were ice cold, like her eyes. She had no interest in me."

Then Sally started laughing. "Ha! Guess who I saw walking around Paramount Studios? Damned if Gary Cooper didn't get his break in the film *The Virginian.* He saw me and acted like nothing happened. All smiles and how-de-dos. He called me 'Baby' and continued back to the set, arm in arm, with no other than Clara Bow. I hear she's the one that convinced the director Victor Fleming to cast him." She smiled wistfully. "I didn't put out and here I sit watching him on the big screen. Shit. Coop sure looked good up there."

* * *

Kay was enamored by the only celebrity she knew, the vivacious Amelia Earhart, or A.E., as she told Kay to call her, who fast became Kay's mentor. It wasn't just A.E. but the fizz of her growing status as a celebrity that impressed Kay. Circling Amelia was her entourage: sister Muriel, journalists, other women pilots, and newbies who needed training like herself. Leading the parade was her husband and public relations guru George Putnam. He set up an exhausting schedule of lectures and endorsements to make her famous. For A.E., it was a means to an end. She was a simple woman. All she wanted out of life was to fly and promote women aviators. Kay admired the lanky woman and was grateful for Earhart's training. Kay noticed on the ground Amelia said little, but up in the air, inside the cabin, she was chatty and enjoyed talking to Kay. "I'm going to fly solo over the Atlantic. Just like Lindbergh. Won't they all have to eat their hats then! Around the world. I want to be the first woman to fly around the world."

Kay was astounded how time had altered for her. Once, life was a series of chores in a day that connected to the seasons and years with little change. Now that Kay was a pilot, time sped to a dizzying pace. What took several weeks on the ground to cross the country only took several hours in the sky. Kay felt compelled to fit more activities in a twenty-four hour period. No longer a janitor, she worked at the airport in the mailroom sorting mailbags for the post office to collect. She was thinking of pursuing her commercial license and applying for a job in the U.S. Postal Service to fly across the country carrying the mail. Foremost, Kay flew at a pace as one obsessed. Her days passed as fast as watching the topography change below her. First, area fields and the growing city of Glendale. Then, the San Joaquin Valley. To fly over the Giant Sequoia grove with their thick red trunks and towering heights made her feel stupendous.

Kay admired Sally's drive and spunk, but A.E.'s energy bypassed Sally by far. On the ground, A.E. was a tornado. The core of her success was that she was a kind woman who was easy to like. She steered her fate to fame by flying back and forth across the country. She starred in stunt shows like the powder puff derby, which showcased female pilots looping in the sky and racing vertically and horizontally for the purpose of breaking records. She joined committees to further women aviators. She became the first president of the Ninety-Nines. A.E. led the pack and consequently persuaded the world that women could fly just as well as men.

Kay recognized there was a type of empowerment cultivated from one who possessed the freedom to explore one's interests. The sky was freedom, and Kay saw a lifestyle in the sky as essential to her being. Thus, AE was more than an ace in the sky. Kay admired her risk-taking attitude. She absorbed the notion that as a woman, Kay could reject the expectations of everyone. Men, women, the Hopi, and society in general wanted her grounded and predictable. She would be Kay Weese the pilot and see where that led her.

In May of 1931, A.E. joined Kay for a flight to Arizona for the weekend. Amelia agreed to use her celebrity status to promote Billy Clark's new airport called the Clemenceau Airport at Cottonwood, the neighboring town of Clarkdale. When Billy Clark shook hands with A.E. and saw Kay, he recognized her instantly. Kay blushed and tried to smile when he took a picture of them standing shoulder to shoulder in front of the painted scroll of *Marvin*. He referenced their last meeting from the Sycamore Canyon adventure and gave her a hug.

"Mighty happy to hear Amelia is teaching you the ropes, Kay. How do you feel when you are up there?"

Kay tried to understand her rejection of the Hopi way of life. Her rejection of a life on the ground and the restrictions of gravity. She had never thought of herself as daring, like the raven floating on the wind. Even though the plane engine was loud to the ears, once she stuffed them with cotton and put on her goggles, she relished the quiet in her mind. Taking off toward the clouds and flying over the slow-moving cars gave her a feeling of accomplishment. On the ground, everything seemed archaic. She grew tired of the dust and sweat that clung. Up in the sky, it was cold. She felt clean. From the patchwork farmlands to the tips of the Rocky Mountains, to be in the sky was miraculous.

She replied to Billy, "I like the view."

Kay passed her test and earned her commercial wings the following summer in 1932. She became an official member of the Ninety-Nines. She enjoyed the company of important female pilots such as Phoebe Omlie who rose in status as Special Assistant for Air Intelligence of National Advisory Committee for Aeronautics. She created a specific purpose for the Ninety-Nines by using WPA funds for her idea of an Air Marking Program. She had a round face and soft eyes and the same electric energy that possessed Amelia Earhart. Phoebe Omlie addressed the men and women who worked and flew at the Grand Central Air Terminal at Glendale.

"No one denies the importance of aeronautics to the present day and the future of the United States of America. What's missing are proper site markings when you're up there looking down. The Air Marking Program will use the talents of the Ninety-Nines to mark the country. Our job will be to divide the states into twenty square miles and plant a marker on a prominent building with the name of the town. That way, visible up in the air, all pilots can see where they are and adjust their bearings if necessary."

Someone in the crowd asked, "What if there's no town? What if we're flying over nothing?"

Phoebe said, "We'll make markers on the ground with stones or brick."

"Sounds like a lot of work."

"You women are going to do that?"

Kay stood up. "I'll help."

Phoebe Omlie smiled and began preparations. She paired Kay with an experienced pilot who had earned her airport transfer license, Laura Ingalls, the distant cousin of the famous author who wrote stories of life on the prairie. Phoebe Omlie assigned them Arizona. While Kay spent the summer getting to know Laura, it quickly became tiresome. She had a bad habit of talking about politics. Kay couldn't have cared less and tried to ignore her. Since Kay was less experienced, Laura treated her like a minion and ordered her about. It was clear to Kay that Laura enjoyed listening to herself talk. She gave speech after speech in the cockpit. Kay stuffed her ears with more cotton, but it didn't quiet Laura's political rants. The hero of Laura Ingalls was the captivating and ambitious Austrian named Adolf Hitler.

* * *

Sally invited Kay to the premier of the film *Flying Down to Rio.* Sally told her to keep her eyes peeled when the chorus danced. She was in one scene, but her participation was enough to get her free tickets and allow her to bring a guest. Kay was flattered Sally thought to include her. As they sat in the dark theater watching Fred Astaire and Ginger Rogers twirl around their fabricated surroundings, Sally nudged her when she saw herself in the chorus sitting on a plane, synchronized and as adorable as any of them. Kay got a kick out of Sally's gratified expression. In that instant, Kay witnessed a landmark event and felt lucky to see her friend's dream come true. Following the applause of the premier, they headed to the cast party. Sally confided to Kay that she thought Vasso and Hermes Pan would help her grow as a choreographer. Perhaps she'd be the lead choreographer of a musical one day.

"What about acting? Don't you want to be the leading lady?"

"Yeah, sure. But not much is happening. I don't get callbacks. I go from one audition to another. So in my spare time I hang out with Vasso. I do whatever she says. I dance with the dancers. I'm surrounded by mirrors and the smell of hard work and discovered it's the world of dancing that makes me happy. I watch Hermes working with Fred Astaire and it's as magical as the end routine. I love working with costume designers. I have visions, Kay. Audacious visions. Oh, I got audacious visions all day long!"

Kay laughed. "That's great Sally."

That's when Connie Vandenberg entered the room through two French doors.

She picked up a glass of champagne from a tray and glided across the room in crinkle taffeta that matched her burgundy lipstick. When Kay spotted her, she was almost relieved. She had thought a lot about Connie Vandenberg and what she would say when they finally met.

Kay was tired of her gut feeling twisted whenever Connie's name was mentioned. Kay did her best to keep calm and resisted touching the red beryl under her dress.

"You two are exactly who I've been looking for."

"Hello, Mother. Party-crashing, I see?"

"You are elusive, daughter. I am disappointed I didn't get an invite to see your film."

Sally said nothing. She pursed her pink lips together and crossed her arms.

"I'll get to the point. Since you won't communicate with me, I was forced to find you. Let's talk about emeralds. To be blunt about it, I want them back."

Sally said, "I told you. George stole them."

Connie ignored her daughter and turned to face Kay. Kay thought about George. He had been linked to Connie for so many years. How tiring it must have been to watch her every move. To the end, he chose to be her partner and thought he had the upper hand. Kay realized George had been played the fool. Did he know? Was that the reason why he consumed opium? How draining to pretend to love someone for years. Did Connie know that? Did she love him or did she pretend, too? Kay felt dizzy by the questions she asked herself. She felt pity for both of them.

A thick streak of gray hair fell from each side of her center part. Kay noticed Connie had changed. Her face was not so painted. Her dress covered her cleavage. She looked like a woman who gave up trying to look twenty years younger. Other than the wrinkles around her lips when she took a puff of her cigarette, she looked better than Kay had ever seen her.

Connie ordered, "Come on you two. Outside where it's private."

They followed obediently through the shimmer of gowns and pressed tuxedos to the balcony. It was a moonless night and the lights of Los Angeles spritely flickered. They were not that far off the ground.

Kay felt the urge to jump off and run.

"I had a nice conversation with my husband, Jonathan."

"Ex-husband," Sally corrected.

"He told me the truth." Connie said to Kay, "You stole the pistol, which had my emeralds smuggled inside and cashed them in. You're lucky you got top price or you'd be sitting in jail." She took out a cigarette from her clutch purse and lit it. Her mouth puckered in the flash of the lighter. Kay stared at her wrinkles. "Giving the cash to Jonathan and Sally doesn't bother me that much. But you aren't family. Your cut belongs to me. I want your 22,000 dollars."

Kay steadied herself. She took a deep breath and said calmly, "You still rum-running for yourself and your sister in Jerome?"

Connie tilted her head. She said nothing, which prompted Kay to continue. "I don't know if Sally told you, but I'm a pilot now. I don't have the 22,000 dollars to repay you. What if I flew to St. Maarten and smuggled back rum for you until the money is repaid? We could work out a deal. Should take, what, a year? Ten runs? I would only fly when the weather's good. Not during the rainy season. Just a few cases at a time, so I don't draw attention. But the details could be worked out."

Connie squinted her eyes and held her pose making her look reptilian. "I no longer have access to the farm. Where would we store the booze?"

"I have flown outside of Chicago several times. There are small airfields outside the city limits. Aren't there places at your hotel where you can hide the rum?"

"They say Prohibition will end soon. I do have friends at the Drake and Palmer House. They might need provisions. On the island, I hear French champagne is available to move."

"Then we better hurry and get your money back. I want to get on with my life."

"George talked about you to me. He said you were tough."

Kay's heart pounded. She wished her heart didn't pine for him. This deal. Would it bring resolution? She shouldn't have taken the emeralds. She shouldn't have bought *Marvin*. She shouldn't have fallen in love with George. Go to jail for theft? No way. She had to protect her status as a Ninety-Nine. She had her commercial license. She would make a living flying. This deal was a temporary sidetrack.

"Did he sleep with you?"

Only a year. She could put up with her. "Not your business, Connie."

Connie was unperturbed. "Prohibition prices will earn more, but even when it ends, I'll legitimize and our smuggled product will become my new import. Hmmm. I like it. Come see me tomorrow at the hotel. We'll work out the specifics."

Connie reached out and touched Sally's forearm with a timid brush of her finger. "Congratulations, daughter. Your dance number was cute." She left them.

Sally blinked at Kay. "You're serious? Your gonna work for her? Don't you see what a slippery slope that is?"

Kay's outburst was like hail pelting down from an angry cloud. "What else could I do? She'd have me sent to jail. How else am I going to raise 22,000 dollars? I just got my new license. I can't have a police record. No one will hire me. It's hard enough that I'm female and an Indian. This deal will be a side job. To shut her up and then say goodbye."

Sally took a step back and shook her head sadly. "My mother will make sure you won't be able to say goodbye."

"It's a risk I have to take."

* * *

Laura Ingalls yelled at Kay to hurry up. "If you're flying in my plane, squaw, you better have the plane checked over and be on time when I say. You're twenty minutes late."

Kay wanted to belt her one, but instead nodded her apology and climbed inside the plane. Kay had just completed her third run from St. Maarten to Chicago. After a day to sleep and regroup, she flew to the Clemenceau Airport in Cottonwood, Arizona to meet up with Laura. Kay folded up her flight map and personal documents she needed to fly to St. Maarten and hid them in her leather bomber jacket.

Smuggling was relatively easy. Three cases of champagne and two barrels of rum were hidden in a secret compartment under the seats in the belly of *Marvin*. Connie paid for the modifications to *Marvin* and added on an extra run to the agreement as reimbursement. Loose inspections revealed nothing, and Kay took off and landed without incident. The pattern was set. She flew from St. Maarten to Miami to refuel. Then she flew six hours to Chicago where Connie had arranged for someone to unload the smuggled cargo. Connie paid for the plane fuel and her traveling expenses and added on a run to compensate herself. Kay was up to twelve runs spread out to accommodate her schedule of marking the state of Arizona with Laura Ingalls and to avoid detection. A year's agreement was beginning to look like two. But at the end of the twelfth run, her debt with Connie would be wiped clean.

* * *

Kay progressed as a pilot. After tolerating Connie Vandenberg and Laura Ingalls for months, she wished for the company of men. When Kay learned that Amelia Earhart broke another record, it incensed Laura Ingalls. She was obsessed with outdoing Earhart's accomplishments.

"I'm flying to South America. I'm going to fly to Chile and back. Set a record. You should come with me and be my co-pilot, Kay."

A snowball's chance in hell.

Kay thought it was a shame. Laura Ingalls was a brilliant pilot. She

wanted to admire Laura and learn from her. But her obsessions obscured her talent like a williwaw blowing into a sunny day. She kept
talking about Jews and how they were the scum of the earth. She kept
Mein Kampf in the plane like a holy book. She was angry and promised
she was going to do something radical for the Nazi party. She hinted
she would fly to Washington, D.C. and drop Nazi pamphlets out of the
plane. Kay felt the pull to join her like a gravitational force. Like Kora,
the Hopi at the park, Laura's wooing was quick and suffocating.

"Join us and become a part of something important."

The only group that mattered to Kay was the Ninety-Nines. She
would not disappoint them. She didn't know much about the Nazi
Party, but they made her think of the red ants in the desert that scrambled about with a harsh sting. Avoiding them was the rule of thumb.
Getting tied up to a group that warped national pride with the rope of
hatred scared Kay.

Laura said, "You'll see. There's a rebirth happening. The Germans
are creating a pristine world. Rising up from the ashes, they will as-
cend and create a new world order." Kay thought Laura sounded like a
speech she had listened to and memorized. "The new Reich. There will
be a war, and I'm going to help them."

"As a spy?"

Laura gripped the yoke and looked sideways at her. "What do you
think of that?"

Kay felt depressed. What a crazy notion. A war? Kay wondered what
she'd do if there was a war. Would she be a pilot for the United States?
She dismissed it. Today was today. She had a plan. Goals. She would
focus on them instead of improbable scenarios. She pressed her finger
over the red beryl on her chest. No one was the wiser. Kay smiled.

She answered Laura Ingalls with the truth. "I think you're nuts."

AFTERWORD

CHAPTER ONE: SALLY

The Roaring 20s was a special time for women to break boundaries and demand their independence. Innovation, music, movies, art, extravagance, and exuberance commanded the decade. Researching the historical climate circa 1927 led me down one road and then another; it was a fun way to get lost. Trying to conceive original characters depended upon a historical vision and then allowing the characters the flexibility to form themselves out of the mental mud I spun.

Thank you, **Barbara Stanwyck** and Flo Ziegfeld girls, for providing me clues about a lifestyle for the fictional character Sally. Vaudeville acts, traveling dance troupes, nightclub dancers, and the high-class Ziegfeld Follies were a part of the Jazz Age across America. Though the Wild West was technically dead by 1927, no one told the 15,000 residents of Jerome, Arizona. The family of a copper baron, miners, cowboys, Native Americans, dance-hall girls, and prostitutes fused with the best technology of the age and imitated the urban environment out in the middle of nowhere with impressive results. Several silent-era actors and actresses transitioned from the chorus line on Broadway by Ziegfeld from 1907-1931. Many westerns were filmed in the area, including nearby Sedona, like **Zane Grey**'s *Call of the Canyon* in 1923. This is where Barbara Stanwyck comes in.

Stanwyck was orphaned at four and was a frequent run-away from foster homes. She became a Ziegfeld dancer at fourteen. That led her to the movie industry and subsequent sixty-year career with 80-plus films to her credit. Imagining Barbara Stanwyck as the driven girl who possessed grit, sex-appeal, and survival instincts were the inspiration for the fictional Sally Vandenberg.

CHAPTER TWO: GEORGE

German Expressionism. What is it? Simply put, it was a movement in art, film, and architecture during the Weimar Republic (1919-1933). At its height during the 1920s, it was a German reaction to the horrors of World War I. Mutilated soldiers returned with haunted eyes, hopeless and depressed. Society as a whole suffered from nightmares more than dreams. Scholarship suggests there was a correlation between the Weimar years of emasculated men who committed depraved sex acts and murders against women, particularly in the 1920s. This reaction to the war might be a link explaining the mindset of a society that allowed Nazi intolerance toward Jews. https://harvardmagazine.com/1997/03/right.lust.html

I turned to the 1927 silent film, *Berlin: Symphony of a Great City*, an impressive composition about urban life during the Weimar Republic. Before the catastrophe of Nazism, Berlin was a mechanized, modern center of Europe. With subways, canals, taxis, factories, and elevators, **Walther Ruttmann** began his film with the sunrise, and clocks chronicled the day of Berliners. I am reminded of ordinary occurrences that are extinct today. Toddlers and children played outside with very little supervision. Milk was delivered to your home in bottles. On the corners of intersections, newsies sold newspapers for five cents and policemen directed traffic. Horses still competed with cars and trolleys for the use of the street. Men pushed brooms while women beat the dust out of their rugs. Water was pitched on front steps for daily scrubbing. Reports were typed and letters were written. People shared rotary phones and were restricted to booths and cords. These details seem meaningless, but they are vital when recreating the time period. In a paralyzed German society after WWI, it is easier to understand how horror came to be expressed on the film screen. Abstract production designs mimicked Surrealism in art. Architecture with exaggerated lines and points replicated the skyscraper. Shadows, nightmares, long staircases, dream sequences, ghoulish villains and pretty, naïve women fed the psychologically damaged. *The Man Who Laughs* is an example inspired by Bram Stoker's classic, *Dracula*. Actor **Max Schrek** plays the vampire Count Orlok, the nocturnal stalker in **F.W. Murnau**'s masterpiece, *Nosferatu* (1922).

Berlin was a stimulating, indecorous urban center. Expressionist German architect **Hans Poelzig** created buildings with a creepy touch. Director was a key pioneer of German Expressionism in the film industry. **Thea von Harbou**, the screenwriter and wife of **Fritz Lang**, had a grip on my imagination while I created the climate of Weimar Germany. The fictional WWI veteran, George Hero, arrived in Berlin in 1922 and stumbled into the world at UFA studios, where Thea's script was directed by Fritz Lang: *Dr. Mabuse: Der Spieler*.

What happened to George's psyche mirrored the country's neuroses displayed visually in Lang's film and substantiated by **Otto Friedrich**'s account of Berlin during the Weimar Republic in his fascinating book, *Before the Deluge*.

How wild were those Berlin cabarets? For descriptions of the venues, the clientele, and street addresses, **Mel Gordon**'s *Voluptuous Panic* was an eye-popper.

CHAPTER THREE: KAY

The *Hopi People* by **Stewart B. Koyiyumptewa, Carolyn O'Bagy Davis**, and the Hopi Cultural Preservation Office was instrumental in learning about the culture of the Hopi. Another imperative work was **James W. Cornett**'s *Indian Uses of Desert Plants.*

To be Hopi is the life-long pursuit to be whole with the universe through traditional ceremonies practiced by a lunar cycle. They revere all things in nature. Their creator is Maasaw, and their matrilineal clan is peaceful. They are migratory farmers and in Clarkdale; their footprint is left by their ancestors, the Anasazi, whose "condominiums" from a thousand years ago, such as Toozigut or Montezuma Castle, are displayed for us in the Verde Valley to admire. Many Hopi live in northeast Arizona, in the four-corner region of the United States. I was fascinated by their expansive knowledge of desert plants and holistic healing. They are expert artisans of silver-making, weaving, and pottery design. Their wooden Kachina dolls are a beautiful insight into their spiritual world.

With 64 books, magazine articles, and 130 films to his credit, **Zane Grey** (1872-1939) was known to many as the father of the Western novel. To understand his influence, I recommend **Thomas H. Pauly**'s biography, *Zane Grey: His Life, His Adventures, His Women*. In his stories, Grey described the grandeur of the Southwest that evoked a desire to visit and a need to protect the vanishing frontier. His heroes were flawed and troubled. He honored the Native American instead of portraying him as a savage. His women were virtuous, strong, and spellbinding. The violence and action of the gunfight were secondary to the enchanted topography Grey conveyed with love. His popular novels contributed to the collective consciousness of the myth of the West well into the 20th century.

Silent films capitalized on Grey's novels. Of the 130 films adapted from his books, a third of the filming locations occurred in Arizona. Reading his most popular novel, *Riders of the Purple Sage*, revealed how descriptive Grey's talents were. There is no doubt for me that Zane Grey's real adventures made his fiction stories authentic. He exemplifies the adage, "write what you know." His descriptions are from someone who rode through the Southwest by horse. I respect the man's adventurous life, and his writing style is nothing short of inspirational. The Western genre in film originates with Zane Grey. His influence spilled into radio shows and television. His film adaptations provided the impetus for many careers including **Shirley Temple**, **Tom Mix**, **Randolph Scott**, and **Alan Ladd**.

Zane Grey's influence abounded in far-reaching ways. While associated with the arid desert landscape, his passion was for deep-sea fishing. He owned patents on fishing lures and held eleven world records in deep-sea fishing. His letters to friend **Ernest Hemingway** linked Grey's attempt to conquer the marlin. Their discussions became the inspiration for *The Old Man and the Sea*.

Today, Zane Grey has schools, subdivisions, and roads named after him. However, by the end of the 1920s, his popularity dipped as a deluge of Westerns circulated in the movie industry. Many careers of Hollywood's best actors participated in the genre of the Western. Connected to the Sycamore Wilderness Canyon is Oak Creek Canyon in Sedona. Sedona was a popular spot for filming and starred several Hollywood heavyweights: **Joan Crawford, Henry Fonda, Glenn Ford, Sterling Hayden,**

Rock Hudson, **Elvis Presley**, **Donna Reed**, **Richard Widmark**, and **John Wayne**. When I wrote the book, I decided on the lost 1925 **William K. Howard** film, *The Thundering Herd*, for the fictional setting.

Alongside **Jack Holt**, **Lois Wilson**, **Noah Beery, Sr.**, and **Raymond Hatton**, the 1925 version was **Gary Cooper's** first uncredited role in film. *The Thundering Herd* is about a trader who uncovers a scheme to blame the Indians for a buffalo massacre. Director **William Howard** remakes the film again in 1933, starring **Randolph Scott**. Sally was besotted by Gary Cooper. Can you blame her?

CHAPTER 4: GEORGE

I give my deepest thanks to the board and members of the Clarkdale Historical Society in Clarkdale, where I volunteered heavily for a year learning about the William A. Clark family and the United Verde Copper Company. An intricate mining system located in the Black Hills of Jerome sent the raw deposits to the smelting plant below in Clarkdale. *Jerome*, by **Midge Steuber**, and the Jerome Historical Society Archives were instrumental in learning about the mining history of Jerome and Clarkdale. The galleries of photos, newspaper articles, books, and older residents who shared their personal histories gave me a valuable history lesson. The founder of a true company town, **William A. Clark** was a rags-to-riches story of the famous copper baron who turned senator. He died in 1925 at the age of 86, leaving an estimated $200 million ($2.5 billion today) and his company town. He established a rail line and a depot in the middle of the desert called Las Vegas. He had nine children from two marriages. His son, **William A. Clark Jr.**, went to Los Angeles and became a rare books collector and the driving force of the Philharmonic

Orchestra. Clark's reclusive daughter, **Huguette**, has become popular because of the excellent biography by **Bill Dedman**, a Pulitzer-prize-winning reporter, entitled *Empty Mansions: The Mysterious Life of Huguette Clark and the Spending of a Great American Fortune*.

The grandson was an aviator who tragically died in the hills outside of Clarkdale when his plane failed to come out of a spin in 1932. Earlier that year, he helped establish the Cottonwood AirField (later known as the Clemenceau Airport) in the neighboring town of Cottonwood. A special guest attended the two-day dedication celebration--Amelia Earhart.

CHAPTER 5: SALLY

Many times, my family and I have ridden up the dirt road to what we fondly refer to as "The Plateau." The stunning vista of the Sycamore Canyon and the Red Rocks of Sedona always impress. It is a place for a campfire and stargazing. It is also the starting point of the story's camping expedition.

Fictional Kay is 19 and experiences a loss of self. In the 1920s, Native Americans generally had three choices for adopting an identity. First, return to the Hopi tribe and "be" Hopi. Second, reject the Hopi tradition and assimilate into the white culture. Third, become a hybrid of sorts, holding on to and existing in the white culture while honoring parts of Hopi traditions discreetly. As Kay figures herself out, she is befriended by an old Apache grandmother who tries to teach her Apache ways. From the 1880s to the 1950s, Yavapai, Apache, Hopi, and Navajo tribes shared traditions because of the forced removal and tribal integration on the reservations. Over the years, tribes blended versions of dances and art forms. While there is a fierce pride in keeping with tribal traditions that are distinct as Hopi or Navajo, Native Americans instinctively bonded with other tribes first before they would bond with whites. This is a generalization, and exceptions are always found. What fascinates me as a social historian is how an individual chooses his or her cultural identity. Native Americans see themselves as unique. They are a minority group trying to be autonomous while surviving in a larger culture. I find their grace and artistry and traditions fascinating. I'm a big fan of Native American photographer and ethnographer, **Edward "Shadow Catcher" Curtis**. From the 1880s to 1930s, Curtis recorded thousands of wax cylinder recordings of music, language, and mythologies of Indian tribes in the Southwest. His expansive photography captures the grace and beauty of Southwest Indians. His photographs are now famous although he had little fame or fortune during his working years. I recommend reading *Edward S. Curtis: Coming to Light* by **Anne Makepeace**. One aspect of the Indian tradition that they all shared was their way of harvesting and use of wild desert vegetation. I recommend **James W. Cornett**'s informative book *Indian Uses of Desert Plants* by Nature Trails Press.

CHAPTER 6: KAY

Early *Glendale* by **Juliet M. Arroyo** was helpful in getting an idea of the Los Angeles Area. Who knew Native Americans camped out in the parks or that there was a union formed by Native Americans objecting to the depiction of Indians in the movies? Another aspect of Los Angeles I was drawn to was the Glendale airport. One of the biggest advancements in the 1920s was in the field aviation for women. One singular organization validated the unconventional woman who dared to fly, the Ninety-Nines, which is still in existence today. The club was created for the purpose of chronicling the achievements of women aviation. I saw photos and posters featuring Native American women aviators and knew my fictional heroine had to make the decision to "aim higher." Flying was the answer to her independent nature. The Ninety-Nines played an active role during the depression with their marking project across America. And there was a female pilot as talented as **Amelia Earhart** who gathered an ignoble reputation as a Nazi spy, **Laura Ingalls**, a distant cousin to the famed writer of life on the prairie. It was a good way to tease the reader's interest in the third book of the series, which will be set during World War II.

In general, my goal was to write a compressed story of three believable characters in the 1920s. Creating a historical climate was the overarching goal. *Inside the Gold-Plated Pistol* is the second novel in a six-part series showcasing the twentieth century with new heroes who have been underrepresented in United States history. I invite you to read the first novel, set in 1900, called *The Knife with the Ivory Handle* (ISBN-10: 0615699855).

Please feel free to visit my personal blog at www.cindybruchman.com

THANK YOU

Since moving to Arizona in 2012, I have had the good fortune to work with great colleagues at Mingus Union High School. Many of them grew up in the Verde Valley and collectively have told me much about the history of Cottonwood, Jerome, and Clarkdale. A huge thank you goes to the brilliant student Violet King. She took part in the editing process and helped isolate sections that needed clarification. To all the members of the Clarkdale Historical Society, I am deeply indebted. To my friends and the inhabitants of Clarkdale, I give my thanks hearing your stories about your historic hometown.

Thank you to Mom, my children, and grandchildren, for your constant support. To my husband, Jimmy, who, if he had a dollar for every time I announced, "I'm working on the novel," he'd be looking at a pile of thousands. We've hiked and camped in the places listed in the novel, and he's listened to me talk about my research for years. I couldn't ask for a more tolerant, devoted partner than Jim Brunot.

Now on to the third installment . . .

CPSIA information can be obtained
at www.ICGtesting.com
Printed in the USA
FFHW020609251019
55765730-61629FF